"Everything has a price, don't you agree?"

Why did she get the feeling this was manipulation at its worst? Yet Danielle had to ask, "What is it you want?"

"A child of my own to whom I can bequeath my fortune. A child born in wedlock," Rafe told her, his expression enigmatic.

She cast him a look of total incredulity.

"It's a question of needs," Rafe offered. "Yours and mine." His gaze narrowed, and his expression assumed an implacability that was frightening. "That's the deal. Take it, or leave it...."

Bestselling Australian author **HELEN BIANCHIN** has a sophisticated, intense writing style and especially enjoys creating commanding, sexy heroes and stylish, passionate heroines. The emotional sparks really fly between her characters, and the sensuality sizzles! In *The Wedding Ultimatum,* Helen explores what happens when an independent woman is forced into a marriage of convenience....

Legally wed,
but he's never said...
"I love you."

They're...

Wedlocked!

The series in which where marriages are made in haste...and love comes later...

Coming next month:

The Blackmail Baby (#2247)
by Penny Jordan

Helen Bianchin

THE WEDDING ULTIMATUM

HARLEQUIN®

TORONTO • NEW YORK • LONDON
AMSTERDAM • PARIS • SYDNEY • HAMBURG
STOCKHOLM • ATHENS • TOKYO • MILAN • MADRID
PRAGUE • WARSAW • BUDAPEST • AUCKLAND

ISBN 0-373-12241-1

THE WEDDING ULTIMATUM

First North American Publication 2002.

CHAPTER ONE

WHAT did one wear to a date with the devil?

Danielle cast a practised eye over the clothes in her wardrobe, made a considered decision, and began dressing with care.

The penthouse suite she shared with her mother in Melbourne's exclusive Brighton suburb had been *home* for as long as she could remember. Luxurious, spacious, it represented the epitome of moneyed class.

But not for much longer. The writing, she reflected grimly, was on the wall. Valued paintings had been sold, secondhand pieces replaced priceless antique furniture. Items of jewellery pawned and auctioned. A standard sedan replaced the stylish Bentley, and creditors circled with shark-like anticipation for the moment bankruptcy was declared and the ultimate mortgaged-to-the-hilt penthouse went on the auction block.

Her mother's collection of credit cards had long reached their ceiling limit, and the La Femme lingerie boutique she jointly owned with Ariane could at best be described as floundering, Danielle admitted wryly as she fixed a diamond stud in each ear. An heirloom that had once belonged to her maternal grandmother, and the only jewellery Danielle had kept.

In less than a week they'd have to walk out of the penthouse, take what personal belongings the bankruptcy court would allow them, seek mediocre rental accommodation, close La Femme, and find employment.

She was twenty-seven, and destitute. It wasn't a good feeling, she reflected as she caught up her evening purse and made her way out to the lift.

It was almost a year since they'd entertained at home, and social occasions were limited to gratis invitations from a few remaining friends loyal to the widow of a man linked to a revered Spanish dynasty.

This evening's meeting was a last-ditch effort to appeal for some form of clemency from the man who owned their apartment building and the shopping complex which housed their boutique. That he also owned a considerable slice of prime city and industrial real estate was immaterial.

In the city's social echelon, Rafe Valdez represented *new money*, Danielle reflected as she reached the basement car park.

An almost obscene fortune accumulated from means, it was rumoured, that didn't bear too close scrutiny.

In his late thirties, he was known to gift large sums to worthy charities, and had, some waspish tongues snidely wagged, used his generous beneficence as an entrée into the élite social circle of the city's rich and famous.

An élite circle to which Danielle and Ariane no longer held access.

Yet she couldn't fail to be aware of his existence. His photo graced the business section of the country's newspapers on occasion, and was reproduced among

the social pages at one function or another...
inevitably accompanied by the latest beautiful young
thing clinging to his arm, a known society matron
anxious to receive media coverage, or any one of several attractive young women who fought for his attention.

Danielle had met him once, almost a year ago, at
a dinner hosted by a so-called friend who, as Ariane's
financial position became known, no longer chose to
extend her hospitality.

Then, she'd taken one look at him and retreated
behind a slight smile and polite but distant social conversation. Self-preservation, she'd qualified at the
time, for to have anything to do with a man of Rafe
Valdez's calibre would be akin to dancing with the
devil.

Now, she had no option. It had taken weeks to
arrange an appointment with him, and it was *he* who
insisted they meet over dinner.

The restaurant he'd nominated was situated in the
inner city, down a one-way narrow lane housing no
fewer than five boutique eating houses. *No parking*
signs were posted on both sides of the lane, and she
circled the block in the slim hope of finding a vacant
space.

Consequently she was ten minutes late...a forgiv-
able time-lag, but not one Rafe Valdez would view
favourably.

She saw him at once, leaning against the small
semicircular bar, and, even as she gave her name to
the *maître d'*, he straightened and made his way towards her.

Tall, dark and dangerous, he bore the chiselled bone structure of his Andalusian ancestors. Eyes as black as sin locked with hers...electric, mesmerising.

An involuntary shiver feathered the length of her spine, and her heart quickened to a thudding beat.

There was something about him that brought all her protective defences to the fore. An intrinsic quality that went beyond the physical impact of the man.

'I hope you haven't been waiting long.'

One dark eyebrow rose slightly. 'Is that an apology?'

His voice was a deep drawl, and held a faint American-accented inflexion.

There was a hint of leashed savagery beneath the sophisticated veneer, an elemental ruthlessness that lent credence to the rumour he'd spent his youth on the Chicago back-streets where only the tough survived.

'Yes.' She met his gaze without flinching. 'If you require an explanation as to *why*...parking was a bitch.'

'You could have taken a taxi.'

'No,' she said evenly. 'I couldn't.' Her budget didn't stretch to taxi fares, and a woman alone didn't choose to use the public-transport system at night.

He lifted a hand and signalled the *maître d'*, whose attentiveness almost bordered on the obsequious as he led them to their table and summoned the drinks steward with an imperious click of his fingers.

Danielle declined wine, ordered a light starter, settled on a main and declined dessert.

'I imagine you're aware why I initiated this meeting?'

He studied her carefully, seeing the pride, the courage…as well as the degree of desperation. 'Why not relax a little, enjoy some food and conversation before we discuss business?'

She held his gaze. 'My sole reason for conversing with you *is* business.'

His faint smile was devoid of humour. 'It's as well I don't possess a fragile ego.'

'I doubt there's anything *fragile* about you.' He was granite, with a heart of stone. What hope did she have of persuading him not to foreclose? Yet she had to try.

'Honesty,' Rafe concluded, 'is an admirable trait.'

The waiter delivered their starter, and she forked a few morsels without appetite, careful not to destroy the chef's artistry as she ate.

All she had to do was get through the next hour…or two. When she left here he would have given her an answer, and her mother's fate as well as her own would be sealed.

She was sure the food was delectable, but her tastebuds appeared to have gone on strike, and she toyed with the main course when it was served, and sipped sparkling mineral water.

He ate with evident enjoyment, his hand movements economical as he utilised cutlery. He looked what he had become, Danielle mused idly…a man among men, attired in impeccable clothes, his suit fashioned by a master tailor. Armani? His deep blue shirt was of the finest cotton, his knotted tie pure silk. The watch adorning his wrist was expensive.

But what of the man beneath the fine clothes? He had a reputation for ruthlessness in the business arena, a power that was utterly merciless on occasion.

Would he be equally inflexible when she voiced her request?

Danielle schooled her nervous system and waited only as long as it took for the waiter to remove their plates before launching into well-rehearsed words.

'Would you be willing to grant us an extension?'

'To what purpose?'

He was going to refuse. Her stomach clenched with tangible pain. 'Ariane can manage the boutique on her own,' she offered. 'While I go to work for someone else.'

'For a wage that will barely cover week-to-week living expenses?' He leaned back in his chair, and indicated the drinks waiter could refill his wine glass. 'It isn't a viable proposition.'

Their debt amounted to a fortune, and one she could never hope to recoup. She met his gaze. 'Does it give you satisfaction to have me beg?'

One eyebrow rose. 'Is that what you are doing?'

Danielle got to her feet and caught up her evening purse. 'Tonight was a mistake.' She turned, only to have her wrist caught in a firm grip.

'Sit down.'

'Why? So you can continue to watch me squirm?' Pink coloured her cheeks, and her brown eyes held a gleam of anger. 'Thanks, but no, thanks.'

He applied pressure and saw her eyes widen with

pain. 'Sit down,' he reiterated with deadly softness. 'We're far from done.'

She looked at her water glass, and for one wild moment she considered flinging its contents in his face.

'Don't.' A silky warning that held immeasurable threat.

'Let go of my wrist.'

'When you resume your seat.'

It was a battle of wills, *his—hers*, and one she didn't want to relinquish. Except there was something prevalent in his dark gaze that warned she could never win against him, and after several tense seconds she sank back into her chair, unconsciously soothing her wrist.

A faint shiver slid over the surface of her skin at the knowledge he could easily have snapped her fragile bones.

'What do you want?' The words slipped out before she could heed them.

Rafe picked up his glass and took a sip of wine, then replaced it on the table as he studied her. 'Let us first discuss what it is that *you* want.'

Wariness curled inside her stomach to mesh with apprehension.

'A wish-list which features a freehold apartment with antique furniture restored, art works, jewellery, all debts cleared.' He waited a beat. 'Ariane's boutique relocated to Toorak Road with an advantageous lease.'

It was impossible to guess his motives, and she

didn't even try. 'That amounts to a considerable sum,' she ventured slowly.

'A million and a half dollars, give or take a few thousand.'

'What did you do?' Her anger simmered beneath the surface, and she held onto it with difficulty. 'Conduct a running inventory?'

'Yes.'

Her fingers clenched until the knuckles showed white. *'Why?'*

'You want me to spell it out?'

He'd sat on the fringes of her life and watched as Ariane's treasured belongings were sold off, one by one? To what purpose?

'I instructed an agent to buy every item you and your mother have been forced to sell.'

What manner of man was he?

One who was prepared to do anything to achieve his objective.

Something which chilled her to the bone.

Danielle examined his chiselled features and felt her nerves stretch to breaking point. *'Why?'*

His gaze was unwavering, and his lips curved slightly in a faint smile that was totally lacking in humour. 'A whim, perhaps?'

A man of Rafe Valdez's ilk hadn't built his life by indulging in a *whim*. Her eyes flashed with barely hidden anger. 'Please. Don't insult my intelligence.'

He lifted the goblet and took a measured sip of wine, then held the stemmed glass and slowly swirled the contents, studying the texture and colour for several seemingly long seconds before shifting his gaze to fuse with her own. 'You intrigue me.'

Something jolted deep inside, and raced through her nervous system with alarming speed. Only a naïve fool would mistake his meaning, and she was neither.

Pride, and sheer courage, enabled her to query with icy calm, 'With almost the entire city's female population, eligible and otherwise—' She paused deliberately, then added with polite sarcasm, 'I fail to see the fascination.'

The waiter served coffee, his smile fixed as he sensed tension thick enough to slice with a knife, then he retreated with polite speed.

Danielle banked down the desire to do the same.

Only the certainty that Rafe Valdez would ignore any histrionics kept her in her seat.

'My father and his father before him laboured in the d'Alboa family vineyards, and considered it an honour to serve such a wealthy landowner.' His gaze never left hers. 'Ironic, wouldn't you agree, that the son of an immigrant peasant has the power to rescue the granddaughter of the revered Joaquin d'Alboa?'

A cold fist closed around her heart. 'This is about *revenge*?'

He smiled, but there was little warmth evident. 'I was merely explaining the connection.'

Danielle watched as he spooned sugar into his black coffee, then lifted the cup to take a measured sip.

His gaze speared hers, his expression enigmatic. 'Everything has a price, don't you agree?'

Why did she get the feeling this was manipulation

at its worst? Yet she had to ask. 'What is it you want?'

'A child of my own to whom I can bequeath my fortune. A child born in wedlock. Who better to conceive and gift me that child than a descendent of the d'Alboa aristocracy?' He watched her features, saw the comprehension, the doubt, then the anger.

'Are you insane?' she demanded in a voice she didn't recognise as her own. 'There are plenty of needy children in the world. Adopt one.'

'No.'

She cast him a look of total incredulity.

'It's a question of needs,' Rafe offered with damnable imperturbability. 'Yours and mine.'

'The hell it is!'

His gaze narrowed, and his expression assumed an implacability that was frightening. 'That's the deal. Take it, or leave it.'

Dear heaven. It was unconscionable. *Wasn't it?*

'Let me get this straight,' she said tightly. 'You're advocating I marry you, and act as a surrogate mother to your child...then walk away?'

He didn't pretend to misunderstand her. 'Not until the child enters the scholastic system.'

She wanted to *hit* him, and nearly did. 'Are we talking kindergarten level, pre-school, or *school*?'

His eyes narrowed fractionally. 'School.'

'Almost seven years, given I should be sufficiently fortunate to fall pregnant immediately?'

'Yes.'

'For which I'll be recompensed to the tune of approximately two hundred thousand dollars for each year?' She paused to bank down the anger and take a fresh breath. 'Paid up front in the manner that free-holds the apartment, clears all debts, restores all Ariane's prized possessions, and resettles the bou-tique?'

'Yes.'

'And what of the years I spend as your wife?'

'You get to enjoy all the fringe benefits of living in my home, acting as my social hostess, a generous allowance.' He waited a beat. 'And sharing my bed.'

She forced herself to conduct a raking appraisal of his features. 'Forgive me, but I don't see having sex with you as a bonus.'

His expression didn't change. 'That's a foolish statement,' Rafe drawled with a tinge of humour. 'For someone who has no experience of me as her lover.'

She banked down wild images of that powerful body engaged in intimacy, and held his gaze. 'Really? Is that knowledge gleaned from superb feminine act-ing and countless ''you were *wonderful*, darling'' compliments?'

'Do you require recommendations as to my sexual prowess?'

Why did she have the feeling she was fast moving out of her depth? 'And when I've fulfilled my side of this diabolical scheme you've devised...what then?'

'Elaborate.'

'After the divorce,' she said succinctly.

'That is something for negotiation.'

'I want all the facts now. Do I get to have visiting rights to my child? Or am I to be cast aside after my use-by date?'

'A suitable arrangement will be made.'

'How *suitable*?' she persisted.

'It is not my intention to banish you from the child's life.'

'But you'll legally limit it to minimum time during the holidays and the occasional weekend.' He'd employ the best legal brains in the country to ensure his influence over the child was total.

'And naturally a pre-nuptial agreement will ensure I walk away after the divorce with nothing.'

'You'll be settled in a suitable residence and maintained with a generous allowance until the child comes of age.'

'I imagine you're prepared to put all this in writing?'

'I already have.' He slid a hand into his jacket pocket and withdrew a folded legal document. 'It's signed and notarised.' He placed it on the table in front of her. 'Take it with you, read it carefully, and give me your answer within twenty-four hours.'

It was unbelievable she was still sitting here. Pride had caused her to attempt to walk out on him once. She knew with certainty the next time he would make no move to stop her.

'What you ask is impossible.'

'You're in no position to bargain with me.'

'Is that a veiled threat to withdraw your offer?'

'Your words. Not mine.' He regarded her steadily. 'This is business. Nothing more, nothing less. I have spelt out the terms. It is for you to accept or decline.'

He was that heartless? She felt sickened as she rose to her feet and collected her purse. If she remained much longer in his company she'd say or do something regrettable.

'Thank you for dinner.' Politely spoken words that lacked sincerity.

Rafe lifted a hand and summoned the waiter. 'I'll see you to your car.'

'That's totally unnecessary,' she responded stiffly, and began making her way towards the entrance.

She acknowledged the *maitre d'*, then stepped out onto the pavement, and she had only managed a few steps when a tall male frame drew level.

'In such a hurry to escape?' Rafe drawled, watching the play of street-lighting on her expressive features.

'You got it in one.'

She reached the corner, turned, and walked as quickly as stiletto heels would allow.

Another block and a half, then she'd be free of him, and she almost counted off the seconds until her car was in sight.

'Goodnight.'

He ignored the obvious dismissal and accompanied her to the small sedan, then stood waiting as she unlocked the door and slid in behind the wheel.

The ignition fired and she attempted to pull the door closed, only to have him hold it open as he leaned towards her.

'Twenty-four hours, Danielle,' Rafe reminded silkily. 'Think carefully. You have much to gain, and everything to lose.'

Then he stood back, and she eased the car out of its parking space and into the flow of traffic.

Damn him. Who did he think he was, for heaven's sake?

Don't answer that, an inner voice prompted as she attempted to focus her attention on negotiating her way out of the inner city.

A marriage arranged to the mutual benefit of both partners wasn't unheard of in this day and age.

The question was whether she could enter into such a business agreement with a man she professed to dislike.

A child. Her stomach muscles twisted into a painful knot at the thought of surrogacy. Rafe Valdez had given his verbal assurance she'd retain an active part in the child's life after the divorce.

Was it too high a price to pay?

First, Danielle determined, she'd have a lawyer peruse Rafe's written agreement.

Then she'd make a decision.

CHAPTER TWO

SEVERAL days later Danielle stood at Rafe Valdez's side in an ornate gazebo situated in the gardens of his beautiful Toorak home and exchanged marriage vows directed by a celebrant in the presence of Ariane and Rafe's lawyer, who acted as witnesses.

The previous week had passed in a blur, each day seemingly more hectic than the last as legal documents were signed and Ariane's affairs brought to order pending the wedding itself.

Soon after signing the marriage certificate, Rafe Valdez would attach his signature to an affidavit authorising payment of all Ariane's debts and the restoration of her previously sold assets.

Wealth was equated with power, and he'd used it ruthlessly to achieve his objective.

Danielle extended her hand for him to slip the wedding ring onto her finger, and her own hand shook slightly as she returned the tradition.

'You may kiss the bride.'

She heard the words, experienced momentary panic as the man at her side cupped her face and covered her lips with his own in an evocative open-mouthed kiss that tugged at something deep inside.

Surprise caused her eyes to widen momentarily before she quickly lowered her lashes, forcing a smile

19

as she accepted the celebrant's voiced congratulations, closely duplicated by Ariane and Rafe's lawyer.

Ariane's hug conveyed maternal concern. The words had all been said, and it lent much to Danielle's resolve that she'd managed to convince her mother that her decision to become Rafe Valdez's wife was not born out of capricious insanity!

Now, however, she wasn't so confident.

Bankruptcy had been averted, a considerable debt wiped, and precious d'Alboa possessions restored. All for a price.

One she was about to begin to pay for.

The man who stood at her side was an unknown quantity. Yet before the night was over she'd share her body with his and engage in the most intimate of physical acts.

The knowledge ate at her equilibrium and almost brought her undone.

During the past week she had seen him once, and that had been in his lawyer's office when she'd attached her signature to the pre-nuptial agreement.

One contact had been made by telephone, informing her of the date, time and place their marriage would take place.

This morning her clothes and personal possessions had been transported to his home, and less than an hour ago she'd driven her small sedan through the tall gates guarding his elegant mansion and entered the spacious lobby with Ariane at her side, where they were greeted by Rafe, introduced to his housekeeper, Elena, and then taken upstairs to an elegant suite.

Attired as she was in a classically styled suit of

ivory silk, the only concession towards *bride* was a single ivory rosebud she held in one hand. Her hair was swept up into a smooth twist, and she wore minimum make-up.

Rafe had chosen formal attire, and she'd taken one look at him, noted the impeccable tailoring, the crisp white shirt, and suppressed the momentary urge to flee.

He had the look of an indolent predator, all darkly coiled strength and indomitable power. Enhanced by a tall frame and an impressive breadth of shoulder. Together with an intrinsic quality that was elemental, primitive.

The celebrant handed Rafe the marriage certificate, offered the customary pleasantries, then left.

There was champagne, and Danielle sipped the sparkling liquid, aware of its potential potency, given that she'd eaten a token slice of toast for breakfast and picked at a salad for lunch.

It seemed superfluous, even hypocritical, to have Rafe's lawyer propose a toast to their union, and a proffered tray of hors d'oeuvres did nothing to tempt her appetite.

Rafe's gaze narrowed as he caught a flicker of concern chase across Ariane's features, and he selected a bite-size portion and deliberately fed it to the woman who now bore his name.

He watched as flecks of gold fire sparked in those dark brown eyes, and for a moment he thought she'd refuse. Certain, had they been alone, that she would have.

The lawyer murmured words Danielle didn't catch,

and Rafe placed his champagne flute down on a nearby table. 'If you'll join me in the study for a few minutes?'

An affidavit requiring his signature following the marriage. Their agreement was a done deal. All *she* had to do was deliver...on a very intimate level, and gift him a child.

She felt her stomach twist into a painful knot. There was no room for second thoughts.

Both Ariane and the lawyer took their leave at the same time, and Danielle watched the small sedan ease down the driveway, followed by the lawyer's late-model BMW.

Rafe turned back towards the lobby, and Danielle followed.

'The master bedroom is upstairs overlooking the gardens and pool, if you want to freshen up.' He indicated the wide curving staircase leading to the upper floor. 'Elena will have unpacked your clothes.' He pulled back a cuff. 'Dinner will be served in half an hour.'

She took it as a dismissal, and was relieved when he turned and retraced his steps to the study.

The Spanish influence was much in evidence, Danielle noted as she made her way towards the staircase.

Pale cream marble-tiled floors patterned and edged with a combination of dark grey, black and a heavy forest-green. Mahogany cabinets hugged the wall space, large urns stood atop marble stands, and original artwork graced the cream walls.

High ceilings in the spacious lobby were offset by

an elegant crystal chandelier suspended above an ornate water fountain. A wide balustraded staircase led to the upper floor.

Guest rooms each with an *en suite*, Danielle determined, a comfortable sitting-room, and there was no mistaking the large master bedroom. His-and-her walk-in wardrobes, a large *en suite* containing luxurious fittings and a spa-bath.

Her toiletries and make-up were neatly positioned at one end of the long marble vanity, her clothing and shoes rested in one of the spacious walk-in wardrobes, and the many drawers held her underwear and lingerie.

She let her gaze skim over the room, noting the pleasing neutral colour scheme in cream and ivory, offset by an abundance of low- and high-set mahogany cabinets, a mirrored dressing-table.

It was impossible not to have her gaze linger on the king-size bed with its heavy quilted spread. Equally difficult to ignore the nervous tension curling painfully in the region of her stomach.

Get a grip, she admonished silently. Rafe Valdez is a man like any other.

However, the prospect of having sex with a man she hardly knew, even within the bounds of marriage, wasn't in her comfort zone.

Yet all she had to do was occupy his bed, and allow him to fuse his body with her own. Maybe if she fell pregnant quickly, he'd leave her alone.

She drew a deep breath and averted her attention from the bed. Maybe she should change? Yet it seemed doubtful Rafe would exchange his suit for something less formal, unless, she determined with a quick glance at her watch, he chose to do so within the next few minutes.

'I imagine you've had time to acquaint yourself with the layout,' a deep voice drawled from the doorway, and she turned slowly towards him.

His jacket was hooked over one shoulder, and he'd loosened his tie. He looked dark and dangerous, his breadth of shoulder impressive without the emphasis of superb tailoring.

'You have a beautiful house.' She couldn't for the life of her call it *home*.

'*Gracias.*' His gaze raked her slender curves. 'Dinner is almost ready.'

She made an instant decision. 'I'll only be a few minutes.' With smooth movements she entered her walk-in wardrobe, selected a dress at random, then hastily exchanged the ivory suit for a red shift, cinched a gilt belt at her waist, touched up her lipstick, then emerged into the bedroom.

Rafe was waiting for her, and she met his brooding scrutiny with equanimity, then preceded him from the room.

Calm, poise. She possessed the social skills to employ both, and she slipped into the familiar role as he seated her at the dining-room table.

There was more champagne, and Danielle toyed with the idea of sinking into a pleasant alcoholic haze, only to discard it in favour of alternating the champagne with mineral water sipped slowly between each few mouthfuls of food.

Elena had prepared a veritable feast, and Danielle attempted to do justice to each course.

'Not hungry?'

She met his piercing gaze and held it. 'Not particularly.'

'Relax,' Rafe bade brusquely. 'I'm not about to sweep all this—' he paused to indicate the china, crystal and various serving dishes '—to one side, and ravish you on the table.'

He watched her eyes widen, then become veiled as her lashes lowered. He was adept at reading an expression, skilled in the art of mind-play.

Most women of his acquaintance would have slipped into seduction mode, teasing with the promise of sensual delights beneath the sheets. Sure knowledge of the sexual act and the mutual pleasure each could derive.

Yet the young woman seated opposite him was consumed with nerves. It was evident in the fast-beating pulse at the edge of her throat, the careful way she consumed each mouthful of food.

'I'm relieved to hear it.' She replaced her fork, unable to face another morsel. The image of that broad male frame sweeping the table's contents to the floor, then crushing her beneath his weight...

'Dessert?'

'No.' Was that her voice? It sounded so calm and controlled, when she was anything *but*. 'Thank you,' she declined.

Elena entered the room, gathered their plates, nodded as Rafe relayed they would take dessert and coffee later, then she left.

The need for conversation prompted Danielle to query, 'At what age did you leave Andalusia?'

One eyebrow lifted. 'Question-and-answer time?'

She toyed with the stem of her glass, her gaze level. In this light she could see the tiny lines fanning out from his eyes, the faint groove slashing each cheek. His facial features bore a chiselled look, and his mouth... She could still feel the touch of his lips as he'd claimed her as his wife, sense the slow sweep of his tongue on hers.

'Anything I know of you amounts to hearsay,' Danielle qualified evenly.

'Will the knowing make a difference?' His faint mockery held a cynical edge, and there was a hardness evident she was loath to explore.

'None at all.'

'Yet you'd prefer to delve into my background, discover what shaped and made me the black-hearted devil I am today,' Rafe drawled. 'With what purpose in mind?' A slight smile curved his lips, but didn't reach his eyes. 'To better understand me?'

Two could play at this game, and she didn't hesitate. 'To separate fact from fiction.'

'Fascinating.'

'Yes, isn't it?'

'Don't stop, Danielle.'

She ignored the warning purr in his voice. 'Fiction tags you as having lived on the Chicago streets, a gang member who walked the wrong side of the law.'

'You believe that?' The tone was silk-smooth and dangerous.

She studied him carefully, attempting to see beneath the façade, aware he would permit only a chosen few to get close. 'I think you did whatever was necessary to survive.'

'A chequered past, hmm?'

To have acquired great wealth in his lifetime meant risk-taking, and living on the edge.

'Is any of it fact?'

His expression didn't change. 'Some of it.'

A street warrior, shoulder-length hair tied back, dark clothes, with attitude. A leader, rather than a follower.

'Somewhere along the way you cleaned up your act. One assumes crime didn't pay?'

He had a hard-nosed cop to thank for turning his life around. A man who had seen potential beneath the bravado, and fostered it, directing the anger towards oriental combat skills in a back-street *dojo*, where discipline was of the mind as well as the body, a spiritualism that channelled energy into something meaningful. That, and one man's faith in his ability to succeed.

He had gone back to school, gained a college scholarship and worked his butt off, graduating with honours. The cop had pulled in a favour that gave him a chance...and the rest was history.

No one knew he'd arranged a retirement package and heavily supplemented the cop's superannuation plan. Or that he'd organised privately funded assistance to provide street kids with sports centres. Centres he personally visited each time he returned to the States.

'Let's just say I made the decision to walk on the

right side of the law,' Rafe declared with thinly veiled mockery.

'That's all you're going to tell me?'

'For now.'

'You didn't answer my original question,' she pursued.

He didn't pretend to misunderstand. 'I was nine years old.' And life, as he knew it, had changed forever. Tension, friction, and a disenchanted father unable to get steady work had eventually split the family. Lack of money had ensured a downhill spiral that fashioned his youth and robbed him of both parents at an early age.

Dusk encroached, and Danielle watched as the day's colours began to fade. There was almost a surreal quality as night descended, an eery stillness before electric lights sprang to life, providing illumination.

'More champagne?'

Danielle met his gaze and was unable to determine anything from his expression. 'No, thanks.'

'We'll move into the sitting-room, and I'll have Elena serve coffee.'

'Does Elena live in the house?'

'No. She comes in Tuesday through to Saturday with her husband, Antonio. Elena looks after the house, prepares and leaves me an evening meal when required, and Antonio takes care of the grounds, the pool, any minor maintenance.'

Danielle took her coffee sweet and black, and she sipped the brew slowly. How long before he would suggest they go to bed? An hour...less?

There was a part of her that wanted the sex over and done with. Another that wished she could slip into an accomplished seduction mode.

'The Toorak boutique is ready for Ariane to move in her stock,' Rafe informed. 'I've organised for transportation tomorrow.'

'I'll ring and arrange to meet her there.'

'Aren't you forgetting something?'

She looked askance at him in silence.

'You're now my wife.'

'Ariane and I are business partners. It wouldn't be fair of me to expect her to set up stock alone in our new premises.'

He examined her features, taking his time before offering comment. 'What if I've made arrangements that preclude you being available to assist your mother?'

'Have you?'

'We're due to attend a tennis party in a private home at two in the afternoon.'

'Which leaves me the morning free to help Ariane,' she responded evenly.

'You have no need to work.'

'You expect me to sit in this house twiddling my thumbs while I wait for you to service me at the end of the day.'

'*Por Dios.*' The oath slipped softly from his tongue. '*Service* you?'

There was a quality evident in his voice that sent apprehension scudding down the length of her spine.

'Given that pregnancy is the main objective, sexual activity should be restricted to my fertile cycle.'

It was impossible to ascertain anything from his expression. As a card player he would be brilliant, she perceived. Yet this was not a game.

'Rather like a brood mare put to stud?'

The softness of his tone was deceptive, and although she was willing to swear he hadn't moved a muscle his posture seemed to have assumed a menacing ruthlessness.

'Why not call it what it is?'

His gaze was unwavering, and it took all her courage not to flinch beneath the silent power emanating from the depths of those dark eyes. Evident was a hard intensity that was almost frightening.

'We occupy the same bed each night,' he said with dangerous softness.

'You intend to enforce conjugal rights?'

'Did you hope that I wouldn't?'

'Yes!'

'Your mistake,' he refuted simply.

'That's—' words temporarily failed her '—barbaric.'

'I doubt you've experienced the true meaning of the word.'

Her chin lifted fractionally, and her eyes blazed with open hostility as she watched his lengthy frame uncoil from the chair.

'You expect me to walk calmly upstairs with you?'

'On your feet, or slung over my shoulder.' He effected a negligible shrug. 'Take your pick.'

'You have the sensitivity of an ox!'

'What did you imagine? Pretty words and romance?'

Danielle stepped ahead of him and made her way towards the elegant staircase. 'I should be so fortunate.'

Careless, foolish words, she chastised silently as she reached the upstairs lobby and turned towards the hallway leading to the master bedroom.

The nerves in her stomach seemed to intensify with every step she took, and she was supremely conscious of the man who walked at her side.

There was no easy way to ignore the large bed, or its significance, as she entered the room.

Did her step falter slightly? She hoped not. Hesitation wasn't on the agenda. Without a word she slipped off her shoes, then she crossed to the set of drawers that held her lingerie. There was a beautiful satin and lace nightgown, a gift from Ariane, which she ignored in favour of a cotton T-shirt, then she moved towards the *en suite*.

A shower might help soothe her soul.

Minutes later she'd shed her clothes, removed her make-up, and pinned up her hair. Then she adjusted the water dial to a comfortable temperature, stepped into the large glassed cubicle, and caught up the soap.

Pride ensured she didn't take overlong, and, towelled dry, she completed the usual ritual, donned the T-shirt, then re-entered the bedroom.

Only to have the breath catch in her throat at the sight of Rafe in the process of pulling the covers from the bed.

A towel was knotted at his hips, highlighting a toned body that displayed an admirable flex of muscle with every move he made.

The olive texture of his skin was offset by a smattering of dark hair at his chest, extending in a single line to his navel. Lean hips and powerful thighs added to a composite that exuded raw strength. Also apparent was a primitive alchemy that fascinated and disturbed in equal measure.

She looked little more than a teenager with her face scrubbed clean of make-up and her hair caught into a careless pony-tail, Rafe mused, his gaze narrowing fractionally as he perceived her hesitation.

CHAPTER THREE

'WHICH side of the bed do you prefer?'

One eyebrow arched. 'Does it matter?'

Oh, *hell*. What could she say? *I'm not very good at this*?

She took the few essential steps to bring her to the edge of the mattress, then she sank down onto it, all too aware of Rafe's actions as he loosened the towel.

She quickly averted her gaze. 'Could you turn out the light?' Was that her voice? It sounded as if she had a constriction in her throat.

'No.'

She was willing to swear she detected a hint of amusement as she felt the faint depression as he sank down onto the bed.

'Let's get rid of this, hmm?'

Danielle felt his hands slide up her thighs as he caught hold of the T-shirt's hem and lifted it over her head. A protest rose and died in her throat, and she crossed her arms across her breasts in an automatic reflex action.

He possessed no such reservations, Danielle observed with resentment, aware of his powerful frame, the sheer size of his arousal.

Dear heaven, how was she going to be able to accommodate him?

A hand closed over her wrist and shifted her arm

away from her breasts, and she lowered her lashes in a protective veil. Only to have him tilt her chin.

'Don't hide.'

The chastisement brought a tinge of colour to her cheeks and her lashes flew wide. 'Maybe you're used to bedding a willing female on short acquaintance,' she vented as he lightly traced the contours of her breast. 'But I'm not comfortable getting intimate with someone I barely know!'

Sensation began deep inside and flared through her body, activating a host of nerve cells in open betrayal. Damn him! Did he know what he was doing to her?

Stupid question! Her jaw clenched, silencing the gasp threatening to escape as he teased one nipple, then rolled it gently between thumb and forefinger.

He lowered his head down to hers and brushed his lips against one temple.

'Please.' There was a catch in her voice as she lifted a hand and indicated a nearby lamp.

'I want to see your reaction to my touch,' Rafe murmured as his mouth trailed down towards her own.

Gentle pressure on her shoulders lowered them down onto the mattress, and she lifted her hands to his chest in an attempt to increase the distance between them. Only to have them freeze as he traced her lower lip with the edge of his tongue, then slipped in to tangle with her own in a slow open-mouthed kiss.

He had the skill to render a woman mindless, and he used it mercilessly in an evocative dance that brought her unbidden response.

She was so caught up with the pleasure of it, she was scarcely aware of the seeking trail of his fingers as they explored her waist, the soft indentation of her navel, then traced a slow path to the juncture between her thighs.

She tensed as he probed the moist cleft, and she was powerless to prevent a protest escaping her throat as he circled the sensitive clitoris, teasing it to such a highly sensitised degree she instinctively pushed against his shoulders.

A hollow groan rose and died in her throat as he eased a finger into the moist orifice, imitating the sexual act itself, and she instinctively arched against the increased pressure of his oral stimulation, alternately exulting in it and hating herself, *him*, for the attack on her emotions.

Danielle almost cried with relief as his mouth left hers and sought a sensitive hollow at the base of her throat.

Not content, he trailed a slow path to her breast, teasing the hardened nipple until she tangled her fingers in his hair and endeavoured to shift his head.

Sensation arrowed through her body as he began to suckle shamelessly before shifting his attention to the other sensitised peak, and she gave an anguished groan as his mouth travelled to her waist, then trailed down over her quivering stomach.

He wouldn't... But he did, holding her flailing hands together with effortless ease as he bestowed the most intimate kiss of all.

She attempted to use her feet, her legs, to buck against him, but he simply adjusted them beneath his weight, locking her into immobility as he took his time gifting a sensual feast that shattered her equilibrium and sent her climbing to heights she hadn't known existed.

Did she cry out? She had no idea of time or place as sensation ruled.

He felt her body quiver, heard the husky sounds emerge from her lips, and he levered himself up over her in one fluid movement, nudging her thighs apart as he eased himself into her.

She was tight, despite his preparation, and he took it slow, feeling her stretch, aware of her momentary panic as she attempted to ease the pressure.

His mouth closed over her own, absorbing her startled cry as he withdrew a little before increasing that initial thrust, repeating the action until she took all of him.

Dear heaven. Danielle swallowed painfully against the feeling of complete enclosure as her muscles contracted around him, causing waves of sensation she was unable to control.

Then he began to move, slowly at first, and she twisted her head from one side to the other as the sensation intensified.

She was conscious of him watching her, and, unbidden, her gaze locked with his as he slowly rocked back and forth, increasing the pace until she was able to accept each long thrust.

It happened again, that powerful, almost excruciating, exquisite spiralling sensation that took her so high she felt as if she was going to fall off the edge of the world.

His climax followed soon after, and she witnessed his attempt at control, watched as he lost it, then marvelled at the extent of his passion.

Nothing she'd experienced came close to the primitive emotion he'd managed to arouse. Raw, spellbinding pleasure meshing with complete fulfilment.

It said much for the man who only hours ago had placed his ring on her finger. Was the seduction deliberate? Or was this his usual *modus operandi* in the bedroom?

If so, she decided shakily, it was little wonder women sought him out.

Seconds later she gasped in shocked surprise as he rolled onto his back, carrying her with him. His eyes were impossibly dark and slumberous with sated desire, and her own widened as his fingers tangled in her hair.

'What are you doing?'

'Removing the band from your hair.'

Free, its length spilled down onto her shoulders, and her eyes widened as he finger-combed the thick mass, then he cupped her face and brought it down to angle his mouth to her own in a kiss that tore at the very foundation of her emotions.

So, he could kiss, part of her brain registered dimly. On a score of one to ten, she'd have to accord him a twenty. And then some. Sensual skill…he had it in spades, aware just which buttons to press to achieve a desired effect.

This is a man you profess to hate, remember? For any number of reasons. Uppermost, the diabolical scheme he'd devised, waiving a considerable debt in exchange for several years of her life...and the gift of a child.

With a muted groan she wrenched her mouth away from his and used her hands to push against his chest.

'I'd like to get some sleep.' She'd had as much of him as she felt she could handle for one night.

Yet even as she voiced the words she felt him swell inside her, his arousal stretching and expanding until he filled her completely.

He couldn't, surely? Not so soon?

'So you shall,' Rafe drawled as his hands moved from her waist to shape her breasts. 'Later.'

He teased the tender peaks, brushing his knuckles back and forth, then he traced a feathery path over her midriff, her stomach, to where they were joined.

Her body jolted as sensation flared, and she clutched his chest as he gently rocked his hips in the first of several undulating movements, each more active than the last until she became lost in an electrifying ride that had her crying out as she reached the brink, then tumbled over the edge in a sensual freefall.

She felt the breath tearing from her throat as she endeavoured to control it, and she had no idea that her skin was flushed with sexual heat, or that her eyes held a dreamy almost witching moistness in the aftermath of passion.

Rafe wanted to roll her over onto her back and take his own pleasure in a series of long hard thrusts that would surely shock. Except he tamped down the desire, equally sure it would leave her hurting.

Unless he was mistaken, she'd had few partners, and unimaginative ones at that.

Or she was a superb actress. Something he very much doubted.

With care he disengaged, then slid to his feet and lifted her from the bed. 'Let's go shower.'

Danielle looked at him blankly for a few seconds, then realisation sank in. 'I'm not sharing a shower with you.'

'Yes,' he drawled softly. 'You are.'

He didn't give her the option to protest further, merely swept an arm beneath her knees and carried her into the adjoining *en suite*.

'Put me down!'

Danielle smote a clenched fist against his shoulder as he reached into the capacious tiled cubicle and adjusted the water-temperature dial.

'Don't you *dare*,' she warned sibilantly as he calmly stepped in beside her and closed the glass door.

He was too close, too intimidating, *too much*. After what they'd just shared she didn't want him in her face, and she particularly didn't want to have him administer to her in any way.

'Isn't anything sacred...even my privacy?' she demanded seconds later as he picked up the soap and began lathering her skin.

'Get used to it,' Rafe drawled as she attempted to twist away from him.

Without success, and she sent him a venomous glare that had no effect whatsoever. 'I hate you!'

Hard fingers closed over her wrist before the fist

she aimed at his ribcage could connect. 'Don't,' he warned. 'You won't win.'

He had the height, the strength, to beat her at anything she chose to fling at him. Although she did possess an advantage or two…one she didn't hesitate to use, only to have him block it in an instant.

A cry of outrage escaped her lips as he lifted her high against him and curved her legs around his waist.

Gone was any hint of amusement. In its place was hard implacability, and she felt a moment's instinctive unease.

'You want to play?'

The query held a silent warning she was too angry to heed, and without thought she lowered her mouth to his shoulder…and bit him *hard*.

Danielle heard his angry hiss at the same time she tasted blood, and she cried out as he hauled her high, her scream of pain very real as he rendered a love-bite to the tender underside of her breast.

When he lifted his head her stunned gaze locked with his for seemingly long seconds, then with deliberate intent he took her mouth with his own in a kiss that was almost savage in its intensity.

Hungry, brazen, he ravaged a primitive assault that lashed at her soul.

Any movement was limited as she was held locked close against him. In desperation she flailed fists against his shoulders, his ribcage, anywhere she could connect…without effect.

How long did it last? Danielle had no idea. It seemed like forever, but could only have been minutes before he released her mouth.

He filled her vision, to the extent there was nothing else, only him. Features harsh in their chiselled perfection, his eyes dark as sin. Compelling, ruthless.

Was this the same man who had indulged her in an evocative journey beyond her experience? A lover who'd fostered her reticence and gifted something so wildly sensuous her body still throbbed from his possession?

She was suddenly conscious of the fine needle-spray of water beating down against his back, her own irregular breathing.

The day, its significance, *Rafe*...it all seemed too much, and she fought against the moisture threatening to well in her eyes.

Oh, for heaven's sake, she silently begged...*don't cry*. Tears, even one, would be a sign of weakness she refused to condone.

Yet she was powerless to still the escape of two lone rivulets that rolled in a warm trail to her chin, and she glimpsed a muscle bunching at the edge of his jaw.

Pride kept her from escaping, and she stood still, fighting the tide of emotion that threatened to fragment any remaining shred of composure.

In seeming slow motion he lifted a hand and smoothed a thumb-pad over one cheek, then the other.

Her mouth felt swollen and slightly numb, and she didn't move as he traced its contours before dropping his hand down to his side.

'Get out of here, *mi mujer*,' he directed huskily.

*   *   *

His voice was the catalyst that set her limbs in motion, and she didn't waste a second stepping out from the shower. Her need to be free of his disturbing presence prompted her to snag a towel and fasten it around her damp form before escaping into the bedroom.

There, towelled dry, the T-shirt in place, she spared the large bed a cursory glance with its tangled sheets, dislodged pillows, and made the decision to sleep elsewhere.

'Don't even think about it.'

Danielle turned at the sound of that silky drawl, and watched him move into the room.

'I don't want to sleep with you.' Bald, brave words, spoken with quiet determination.

'Correction…you don't want to have sex with me.' He waited a beat. 'In this instance, *sleep* is the operative word. And we share the same bed.'

'No.'

'I wasn't aware I gave you an option.'

Anger flared anew. 'Go to hell!'

His gaze speared hers. 'Believe you don't want me to take you there.'

'Oh?' She was like a runaway train on a track leading to disaster. 'And what—' she flung an arm in the direction of the *en suite* '—was that happening in there? A *guy* thing? Or a lesson in subjugation?'

'You have a foolish mouth,' Rafe warned with chilling softness.

'If you wanted a meek, subservient wife you should have married someone else.'

'Instead, I chose you.' He paused, spearing her angry gaze with hateful ease. 'The purpose is specific...or have you forgotten so soon?'

Danielle tore her gaze away from his. 'If you touch me again tonight I'll—'

'Fight me to the death? Scratch my eyes out?' He leant over the bed, straightened the pillows and hauled up the bedcovers. 'Be warned, I'm a light sleeper.'

'What does that have to do with anything?'

'A warning, should you decide to go sleep somewhere else in the middle of the night.'

'You can't—'

'Watch me.'

'You're nothing but a tyrannical bully!'

He unfastened the towel knotted at his waist and tossed it aside. 'I'll wear only so many insults.' He slid in beneath the covers. 'Get into bed, Danielle.'

'What if I don't?'

Dark eyes pierced hers. 'I'll put you there.'

A lock of hair fell forward onto her cheek, and she tucked it back behind her ear in an involuntary gesture.

Capitulation was born out of wisdom...for now. Although she didn't feel particularly wise as she reluctantly slid into bed. In a final gesture of defiance she turned her back towards him and hugged the edge of the mattress.

Something that gave her little satisfaction, for he merely snapped off the light, plunging the room into darkness, and she lay there tense, listening to his breathing slow into a steady rhythm.

How could he slip so easily to sleep? Too much

practice in the face of danger? Or a finely tuned mechanism that permitted him to wake at the slightest sound, the faintest move?

What had he witnessed in his youth to have created such a hard exterior? Had fate dealt him such a difficult hand that he had no heart?

Could the right woman change his perspective? Could *she*?

Dear lord, what was she *thinking*? Her sole purpose in his life was to produce a child, then, following the requisite time span, move on.

Besides, what woman would willingly welcome a man of Rafe Valdez's calibre into her life?

Many, she admitted with obvious reluctance. The size of his cheque-book guaranteed obsequious adoration from the trophy wife prepared to be both gracious hostess and a seductive mistress. In all probability, willing to gift him a child.

So why *her*, when he could have chosen any one of several young women?

Because she refused to conform, and frequently opted for confrontation? Even to her detriment?

Or was it simply *circumstance*, as he'd claimed? Let's not forget the d'Alboa lineage, she added silently.

Did it really matter?

With a faint sigh she attempted to ease her tense body. Curled into a tight ball on the edge of a mattress was not her normal sleeping position.

She was already beginning to feel the tightness in several muscles. And she hurt, inside and out. Her breast ached from his retaliatory bite, and she ran her tongue over the tissues inside her mouth where he'd heartlessly ground them against her teeth.

It would be so easy to indulge in a crying jag. Wasn't there some analogy that credited weeping as a release to soothe the soul?

One solitary tear spilled and ran warmly down her cheek, and she brushed it away in angry rejection.

It was a while before she slipped into an uneasy sleep, from which she stirred to Rafe's touch as early dawn fingered the day's first light through the shuttered windows.

His sexual appetite ran to night *and* morning? Maybe if she simply lay there...

Fool, she accorded minutes later as warmth flooded her veins. He played her like a finely tuned instrument, seeking an unbidden response that had her clinging to him like a craven wanton.

Afterwards she slept, and when she woke it was morning, the space in the bed beside her empty.

CHAPTER FOUR

DANIELLE rolled over, checked the time on the digital bedside clock, then she slid swiftly to her feet, collected her cellphone and punched in the requisite digits to connect with her mother.

'Good heavens, darling. I don't expect you to come in this morning,' Ariane protested. 'I can manage quite well on my own.'

'With two of us, we'll be able to sort the stock in half the time,' Danielle said lightly as she crossed to the walk-in wardrobe, selected jeans and a singlet top, then she tossed them onto the bed before collecting fresh underwear.

'Are you sure Rafe won't object?'

She tucked the small phone beneath one ear and began pulling on briefs. 'I don't see why he should,' she managed evenly. 'As far as I know there are only plans for the afternoon, and I'll be back in time.'

The jeans came next, and she stepped into them, then manoeuvred them up over her hips.

'Shall I collect you? I have the car, remember?'

Oh, hell. She'd forgotten. 'OK. I can be ready in twenty minutes. I'll meet you at the gate.' In one fluid movement she tugged off the T-shirt, then gave a yelp in surprise as the cellphone was taken out of her hand.

She made a quick lunge to retrieve it. 'Give me that!'

Rafe merely put the phone to his ear. 'Ariane? We'll meet you at the boutique.' And disconnected the call.

Danielle spared him an angry glance. 'What do you think you're doing?'

'I believe it's called helping out.'

She became aware of her semi-nudity, and hurriedly turned away from him as she reached for her bra, fastening it in record time before pulling on the singlet top, and slipping her feet into trainers.

'It isn't necessary,' she flung over one shoulder and she entered the *en suite* and closed the door.

He was still there when she emerged. She'd swept her hair into a knot atop her head, and her only concession to make-up was a touch of gloss to her lips.

'You've had nothing to eat.'

He too was attired in jeans, trainers, and a polo shirt that hugged his muscular shoulders and emphasised powerful biceps.

She caught up her cellphone, collected her purse and sidestepped him. 'I'll grab something later.'

'I shall see that you do.'

'I dislike tyrannical men.'

'I've been called much worse.'

'Without doubt,' she responded with an edge of mockery.

She reached the head of the stairs and ran lightly down to the ground floor, aware he followed close behind her.

The garage was accessed via a hallway leading off from the lobby, and minutes later he eased the gleaming top-of-the-range Jaguar through the gates, then headed towards Toorak Road.

The positioning of La Femme was ideal, situated in a small U-shaped modern complex comprising seven upmarket shops and a boutique café specialising in fine coffee and gourmet food.

Danielle had to give Rafe his due, for he'd consulted with Ariane over shop-fittings, ordered what she'd requested and ensured the re-fit was completed in time to orchestrate the shift of stock.

Not only that, in Ariane's eyes he'd changed from ogre to champion by sanctioning an order of new French imports commensurate with patrons' expectations.

With their line of credit reopened and Rafe Valdez's financial backing, the attitude of wholesalers' representatives had undergone a dramatic change.

New stock had arrived by courier yesterday, and a further delivery was promised for tomorrow.

'Just drop me outside,' Danielle instructed as Rafe slowed the car and pulled into the kerb. 'I'll get a taxi back.'

He cut the engine and followed her onto the pavement, arching an eyebrow as she cast him a studied glare.

'There's no need for your personal inspection.'

'On the contrary,' Rafe drawled. 'I make it a habit to check all my investments.'

The gold sign-writing on the shop window looked good, and she could see Ariane behind the plate glass checking boxes of stock.

Was it Danielle's imagination, or did her mother's

gaze linger a little too long? What was Ariane looking for? A sign Rafe Valdez had mistreated her daughter?

Danielle could have reassured there weren't any. At least, none that was visible.

'Shall we get to work?'

She cast Rafe a cursory glance. 'You intend to stay?'

'You object?'

'Of course not,' Ariane responded with a ready smile. 'The stock will need to be sorted according to style, colour and size. I'd like to organise the display cabinets and attend to the window dressing.' She referred to the floor plan and the list they'd compiled on Friday. 'I've already made a start. Danielle, you search and sort, and I'll stack.'

'What would you like me to do?'

'Fetch and carry,' Danielle declared, crossing to one of the large boxes and slitting open the heavy masking tape.

It took a while to unpack all the boxes, then stack individual packets in coded order in the numerous large pull-out drawers contained in waist-high cabinets lining each opposing wall.

'I'll go fetch drinks and something to eat,' Rafe indicated, breaking from the task of collapsing yet another large box. 'Any preferences?'

'I packed sandwiches and brought bottled water,' Ariane informed. 'They're in the fridge out back.'

Danielle rose to her feet from a kneeling position, and stretched her arms. 'I'll get them.'

'We'll join you, darling. It'll be nice to sit down for ten minutes.'

There wasn't a great deal of spare space in the storeroom. Shelves lined the walls from floor to ceiling, and there was a small table and two chairs, and a servery cabinet which held a sink, crockery, cutlery, an electric kettle and a small microwave.

Danielle retrieved sandwiches and drinks and set them on the table.

'All the grunt work is done,' she declared as she fetched glasses and began filling them with water.

'Thanks to you both,' Ariane agreed with satisfaction. 'There's just the display cabinets and the window.'

For the past two and a half hours she'd been supremely conscious of Rafe's presence. The fluid ease with which he moved, the occasional brush of his fingers against her own as she took each stack of packets from his hand. The way his gaze lingered a fraction too long.

It unsettled her. Worse, it evoked a vivid memory of what they'd shared through the night. And would again. The purpose was evident in his eyes, a deep slumberous passion that held its base in sexual desire...nothing more, nothing less.

The sandwiches were delectable, and Danielle elected to tidy up while Ariane began on the window. Rafe remained where he was, and she turned towards him.

'There's no need for you to stay. I'll make sure I return to the house in time to shower, change and be ready by two.'

He reached out a hand and tucked a stray lock of hair behind her ear. 'No.'

Her pulse quickened, and there was nothing she could do to quell the heat coursing through her veins. Each separate nerve end seemed to flare into vibrant life at his touch, and she silently cursed him anew.

With quick, economical movements she rinsed glasses, dried and replaced them in the cupboard, then she crossed the storeroom, aware he followed close behind her.

With care, Danielle created an artful window display with tulle and satin ribbons, then dressed three mannequins in La Perla. A large illustrated catalogue was propped against an antique satin-padded chair, over which she draped a suspender belt in French lace.

A concentrated scrutiny, a few adjustments, and Ariane conceded it perfection.

All that remained was the need to dress the interior glassed showcases, which Ariane assured she could easily handle on her own.

'Are you sure?'

'Of course, darling. Besides, you probably have plans of your own for the afternoon.'

The tennis party, Danielle remembered with dismay. Her first entrée back into the social scene. A quiet afternoon spent lazing on a lounger by the pool with a good book was infinitely preferable to a few energetic games of tennis. Not to mention bearing the circumspect scrutiny of the social set.

'Yes, we do,' Rafe concurred, not missing the fleeting cloud that momentarily dulled her eyes, nor divining its cause.

'In that case, you must leave.' Ariane checked her

watch. 'It's almost one.' She leant forward and brushed her lips to Danielle's cheek. 'Have a good time. Thanks for your help.'

'I'll see you tomorrow.'

The boutique had come alive, and it looked good...really good, Danielle conceded as she slipped into the passenger seat of Rafe's car.

'I'll drop you off in the morning, then arrange for a car to be delivered to you through the day,' he indicated as he pulled out into the stream of traffic.

She didn't particularly want to accept anything from him, but a car was a necessity. 'Thanks.'

'I've suggested Ariane interview prospective staff to fill in part-time when you aren't available,' he continued, and she rounded on him at once.

'What do you mean—*not available*?'

'You'll accompany me whenever I travel on business. There will also be occasions when you'll need to take time off to attend an early-evening function, or a specific charity luncheon,' Rafe informed smoothly, aware of her mounting anger.

'La Femme is a priority.'

'Your first loyalty is to me.'

'My apologies,' Danielle offered facetiously. 'For a moment I forgot that I'd been bought and paid for.'

'Don't push it.' His voice was silk-smooth and dangerous, and succeeded in feathering apprehension down her spine.

Lunch was a delicious paella, followed by salad greens, and it was almost two when Rafe pulled into a familiar driveway and parked at the rear of a line of cars.

Lillian and Ivan Stanich.

Danielle's heart sank. By attending this particular soirée, he was throwing her in at the deep end. She could imagine the guest list, and had it confirmed as they entered the house.

'Rafe, darling.' Lillian went with the air-kiss routine, then she took a step towards his partner, only to pause momentarily as recognition hit. 'Danielle?'

'My wife.'

The recovery was swift. 'How delightful. Congratulations.'

Really? How long would it take for the gossip scoop to circulate? Five minutes? And who will be the first to try ascertaining the story behind the news? Or had the rumour mill already begun with the relocation of La Femme?

'Come through to the terrace and join everyone for drinks. Ivan has already organised the games roster.'

Danielle summoned a smile and suppressed the silent wish to be anywhere else but *here*, and followed in Lillian's wake.

Not one to miss an opportunity, the society doyenne clapped her hands to gain her guests' attention and announced Rafe's marriage, adding with a delighted chuckle, 'We're the first to know.' Turning towards Rafe, she offered a wicked smile. 'You've kept this very quiet, darling.'

'As I do most things in my personal life,' he drawled in response.

'So you're not going to enlighten us with any details?' Lillian queried coyly.

He caught hold of Danielle's hand and brought it

to his lips. His eyes were dark, their expression unreadable, then after a few electrifying seconds he lowered their linked hands to his side and met Lillian's avid gaze.

'No.'

There was a suspended silence during which it would have been possible to hear a pin drop, then Lillian spread her hands and gave a tinkling laugh.

'This calls for a celebration. Ivan must fetch some champagne.'

Danielle made a surreptitious attempt to free her hand without success. In a deliberate gesture she leaned towards him and uttered in a quiet voice, 'Just what are you playing at?'

'Solidarity.'

'A *united we stand, divided we fall* stance?'

'Yes.'

'You surprise me.'

'Why?'

'I imagined you'd have no hesitation in throwing me to the wolves.'

His gaze was direct, his voice as smooth as silk. 'I take care of my own.'

But she wasn't *one of his own*. At least, not really.

There were, of course, voiced congratulations, and she kept a smile pinned firmly in place as she was greeted by former friends whose enthusiasm didn't fool her in the least. These were people who'd turned their backs when the chips began to fall, whose invitations had become remarkably absent, and who had quickly refused to acknowledge Ariane or herself in any way.

Now that she was Rafe's wife, they were eager to renew their friendship. An act which she viewed with extreme caution and a degree of cynicism

'*Querido,*' a feminine voice purred.

Danielle turned slightly to face a statuesque blonde who was perfection from head to toe. Sex appeal, more than her share of pheromones, and the self-assurance of a modern-day Circe.

'Cristina,' Rafe acknowledged.

The blonde switched her attention to Danielle, and proffered a superficial smile. 'How dare you steal him away from me?'

It was spoken in jest, but there was no humour in those cool grey eyes.

'Perhaps you should ask Rafe?'

A suggestion which didn't go down at all well, and unless Danielle was mistaken a war had just begun.

'One of your many conquests,' Danielle acknowledged as she sipped champagne.

'We dated on occasion.'

It was as well Lillian and Ivan began marshalling players onto the two tennis courts adjoining their property, and Danielle found herself paired with Rafe against Cristina and her partner.

Tennis whites were obligatory, and her short pleated skirt and singlet top didn't come close to the designer gear Cristina wore.

What was meant to be a friendly game became highly competitive as the beautiful blonde deliberately set out to trounce Danielle off the court.

Something she refused to allow to happen, and it

said much for her own skill at the game that she managed to return almost every shot.

As expected, Rafe was a superb player, and, aided by height, strength and a killer serve, they completed the first set with a two-game lead.

It was a knock-out tournament, and it came as no surprise when Rafe took them into the final to win by a narrow margin.

He looked as if the afternoon's exercise had been no more strenuous than a walk in the park, whereas another set would have killed her!

Barbecued prawns and kebabs were served at eight with a variety of salad greens, followed by coffee.

'Danielle, you really must join the girls at next week's luncheon. I'll forward an invitation.'

The *girls*, huh? There was a certain irony in the fact that where Lillian led, others would follow. 'How kind.' She would decline when the invitation arrived, citing her commitment to La Femme.

There were a few charities she'd willingly support...by gifting a cheque, rather than by putting in an appearance among women who displayed such superficial artificiality.

Rafe saw the polite mask and was aware of the effort it cost her to project a pretence. She looked fragile, and there were faint shadows beneath her eyes.

Hardly surprising, given he'd kept her awake for much of the night.

With care he drained the last of his coffee, and crossed to her side.

'Ready to leave?'

'Yes,' she responded simply, wanting only to get out of here. She'd had enough, she was tired, and bed had never looked so good.

Except *bed* meant sharing intimacy with a man who'd wreaked havoc with her ambivalent emotions. There hadn't been a moment through the day when just one glance at him brought forth a vivid image of the previous night. That mouth, those hands... Something stirred deep within at the thought.

Dangerous thoughts. It would be easier if he was an inept lover, more focused on his own pleasure than hers.

Minutes later they thanked their hosts and began bidding fellow guests goodnight.

Danielle slid thankfully into the car, and laid her head back against the cushioned rest.

'You played the game well.'

She turned her head to look at him. 'Are we talking tennis, or the social deal?'

He fired the engine and eased the car around the semicircular driveway, then gained the street. 'Both.'

'Ah, a compliment.' It was impossible to avoid a trace of mockery.

The drive was a short one, and it seemed only a matter of minutes when Rafe drew the Jaguar to a halt inside the garage.

All she wanted to do was shed her clothes, take a shower, then slip into bed...to sleep.

Except there was as much chance of that happening as flying over the moon, she perceived as Rafe followed her into the shower.

'Isn't this carrying *togetherness* a bit too far?'

He trailed fingers across her shoulders. 'You've caught the sun.'

This close, she was supremely conscious of his powerful frame, the musculature of his chest and shoulders. And his unmistakable virility. It was an overwhelming force that swamped her senses.

Eyes front, an inner voice taunted. Better yet, turn away from him. Caution warned that might invite more than she was prepared to deal with.

She noticed a thin white diagonal scar on his left ribcage. Non-surgical. The careless slash of a knife blade?

Her head lifted, and she paused to examine a scarred indentation close to his collarbone that looked suspiciously like a bullet wound.

There was also an unusual oriental symbol tattooed on his upper right arm, and she wondered why he'd kept it, rather than have it cosmetically erased.

'Battle scars?' she posed, meeting his steady dark gaze.

'From my less than salubrious past?'

'How *less than salubrious*?'

'Do you really want to know?'

Her expression didn't waver. 'It's part of who you are.'

There were parts of those youthful years he refused to share with anyone. The edge of his mouth took an upward twist. 'How…profound.'

She caught up the soap and attempted to ignore him. An impossibility, given the size of the shower cubicle and his proximity.

Seconds later the soap-bar was taken from her

hand, and she tossed him an angry glare. 'Must you? A seduction scene isn't high on my list of priorities.'

'Why not close your eyes and enjoy?'

Something that would prove a sure path to disaster. Already her body was beginning to respond to his touch, with warmth spreading through her veins, disrupting her pulse-beat.

'I don't want to go there. At least, not tonight.'

He caught the slight catch in her voice, sensed the fragility evident, and slid his hands to her shoulders. 'That bad, hmm?'

She ached, everywhere. It was ages since she'd worked out, months since she'd last played tennis. Gym membership had been one of the first things to go, along with sports' club fees.

Dear heaven. His fingers were working magic, easing out the kinks, soothing tight muscles. The temptation was very strong to do as he suggested and just close her eyes.

It would be wonderful to turn into his arms and rest against him, to feel his palms skim over the surface of her skin and soothe away the tension of the day.

Where had that come from? Rafe Valdez had only one objective, and that was to satisfy his libido, and to father a child.

With a silent derisory groan she moved out of his grasp, exited the shower cubicle, snagged a towel and fixed the ends together above her breasts, then emerged into the bedroom.

Rafe joined her just as she was pulling a T-shirt

over her head, and his gaze narrowed at the faint dis-
colouring blemishes marring her skin.

It wasn't his practice to harm, and he had to ask
why it bothered him this woman should bear the
marks from his touch.

She possessed a slender lissom body, slim legs displaying good muscle definition, and there was a fluid
grace in the way she moved.

'Why a cotton-knit T-shirt as sleep-wear, when you
have access to various luxury creations in silk, satin
and lace at La Femme?'

Danielle turned her head and sent him a challenging glance. 'Perhaps I chose this—' she paused and
indicated the fabric with an index finger '—as a turn-
off.'

'Since whatever you wear won't stay on long,'
Rafe drawled, 'it hardly matters.'

She chose not to answer, and merely pulled back
the covers and slid into bed, aware as she did so that
he crossed the room, snapped a switch and plunged
the room into darkness.

Seconds later she felt the faint depression of the
mattress as he slipped in beside her, and she tensed,
waiting for the moment he'd reach for her.

Except the minutes dragged by, and she closed her
eyes as tiredness overcame any desire to conduct a
post-mortem on the day's events.

It was in the early pre-dawn hours that she struggled against wakefulness as male hands caressed her
thighs, then gently tugged the T-shirt over her head.

Her murmured protest had little effect as Rafe gathered her close and nuzzled the sensitive hollow beneath her earlobe.

Danielle pushed against him, then groaned out loud as his mouth trailed to her breast, lingered, then traced a downward path.

She tasted of woman, warm and musky, and he stayed there a while, savouring her, cradling her hips as she lost control.

It was with ease he nudged her thighs further apart, then he plunged deep inside, aware of the way she expanded to take him, and heard the breath hiss from her throat as he began to move, rocking gently back and forth until she dug her fingers into his shoulders and matched his rhythm.

Afterwards they slept, then rose to shower and dress.

CHAPTER FIVE

BREAKFAST was a leisurely meal eaten al fresco on the terrace, and Danielle filched the fashion segment of the newspaper while Rafe studied the financial pages as they enjoyed a second coffee.

He looked relaxed and at ease, bearing a pantherish grace as he leant back in his chair. His dark hair was well-groomed, his face freshly shaven. His shirt was unbuttoned at the neck, and his jacket and tie were spread over a nearby chair. A briefcase and laptop sat on the floor close by.

The successful corporate executive, she mused idly, who wielded power and authority with incontestable right.

There was an inflexible quality evident, a hardness that came from the will to survive against the odds.

At that moment he looked up, and she met his steady gaze.

'If you've finished, we'll leave.' He drained the last of his coffee, then rose to his feet, attended to the two top buttons of his shirt, reached for his tie and fastened it, then he shrugged into his jacket.

It was almost eight-thirty when he brought the car to a halt adjacent to the boutique.

'I have a business dinner this evening.'

Danielle unclipped the seatbelt and reached for the door-clasp. 'So don't wait up?'

He ignored the faint cynicism. 'A car will be delivered to you this afternoon.'

'Thank you.' She slid to her feet and closed the door, watching as he eased the Jaguar back into the flow of traffic.

Danielle unlocked the boutique and discovered Ariane had already arrived, and together they effected a few minor changes, checked the stock list, before moving on to discuss a layout for their proposed catalogue.

The morning's trade was brisk as women stopped by to check out the new premises and the range of stock. Some were merely curious, others were there to purchase.

A few former clients wandered in, bought, and attempted to repair a severed friendship.

It was, Danielle determined, superficial behaviour at best and motivated by a need to establish favour with her powerful husband.

Integrity ensured she project a polite façade. Business was *business*, and it was a matter of pride the boutique should succeed.

Lunch was a fifteen-minute break each, taken in succession, and there was a stock delivery midafternoon.

Soon afterwards a sales manager presented her with the keys to a BMW parked out front. An hour before closing time Danielle signed for a certified document delivery from a prominent city bank. Inside was a portfolio containing cheque-book, ATM and credit cards in the name of Danielle *Valdez*.

Rafe, she perceived. Keeping his end of the bargain.

It shouldn't irk her so much, but it did. She attempted to analyse why, and attributed the blame to Rafe having taken control of her life. Except honesty compelled her to admit she was responsible for giving him that option.

As if she'd had a choice!

Who, in their right mind, would settle for bankruptcy and poverty when offered the opportunity to grasp an advantageous financial alternative?

Yet it came with a high price. Would *she* be able to keep *her* end of the bargain?

Dammit, introspection was of no benefit at all, she determined, and busied herself replenishing drawers with stock from the back room.

At five-thirty they closed up, checked the day's takings, and uttered a quiet whoop of delight at the figures.

It was after six when Danielle entered Rafe's Toorak home, and on a whim she shed the tailored business suit she wore to work, donned a swimsuit and headed down to the indoor pool.

The land out back had been carved away to incorporate a lower level devoted to a private gym, indoor pool, a spacious shower and bathroom.

The water was cool, and she stroked several laps before emerging to snag a towel, then head for the shower.

Dinner was a chicken salad Elena had left prepared in the refrigerator, and accompanied by chilled juice it made for a satisfactory meal.

The house seemed much too large for one person...correction, two. The downstairs rooms were spacious, and ideal for entertaining. The formal dining-room held no fewer than twenty-two chairs positioned around a long rectangular table. The formal lounge held comfortable sofas enough to seat a similar number.

Danielle collected a glass of chilled water and settled herself in front of the television, viewed a few of many programmes available via satellite, then retreated upstairs to bed at ten-thirty.

At what time would Rafe return? She plumped her pillow and told herself she didn't care. The later the better, for then hopefully he'd be tired and not bother her.

Fat chance, she protested silently as she emerged from the depths of sleep to the brush of his lips against the curve of her shoulder.

His mouth became an erotic instrument as he brought her to wakefulness, and in the darkness she clung to him, qualifying her own satisfaction as a pleasant fringe benefit in an otherwise diabolical scheme.

It was when they shared breakfast next morning that Danielle remembered the BMW.

'Thanks for the car.' She waited a beat. 'And organising details with the bank.'

Rafe drained his coffee and poured himself another. 'I intend that you shall.' He speared her a musing glance. 'Thank me.'

His meaning was unmistakable, and she hated the warmth heating her cheeks.

'Delightful.' His voice was a teasing drawl. 'A woman in today's age who can still blush.'

'It's a knack you have.'

'An integral part of my charm,' he conceded with a faint edge of mockery.

She opted to forgo another coffee and rose to her feet. 'I told Ariane I'd be early.'

'Hasta luego.'

The days were busy as the boutique flourished, much to Danielle and Ariane's delight. Quiet times were rare, and they interviewed several women before selecting one as necessary part-time staff with the capability of temporary full-time work as and when Danielle or Ariane might be absent.

At night there was Rafe.

The pattern during that first week followed an increasingly familiar routine. They ate in, Rafe secluded himself in the study with his laptop and rarely emerged much before ten.

Danielle utilised a desk in one of the spare rooms and checked figures and stock numbers, searched numerous internet sites, solely for the purpose of streamlining La Femme and providing clients with the ultimate in luxury lingerie.

Proofs for the catalogue were in place, but she wanted to be sure the assemblage couldn't be bettered before handing it all to the printer.

Rafe appeared to be one of the fortunate few who could apply optimum effort to a hectic work schedule with a minimum of five hours' sleep. Less, given the regularity with which he reached for her through the night.

Each time made it more difficult for her to remain emotionally distant from him. He had the touch, the skill, and he applied the time to ensure her pleasure matched his own.

Saturday dawned bright and clear, the sun's heat soaring with high humidity levels guaranteed to try anyone not blessed with the comfort of air-conditioning.

Traditionally, a Saturday was one of the busiest trading days of the week, with those who worked office and professional hours utilising part of the day to shop without having to cram everything into a lunch-hour.

It was an excellent day to have Leanne, the assistant Ariane had hired part-time, come in to work. Especially as Danielle needed to leave an hour before closing time.

A dinner party, Rafe had informed the previous morning, to be held at the home of a prominent social hostess.

It didn't help that Danielle was delayed due to a severe traffic accident, or that it took time for a uniform to appear and redirect banked-up traffic.

As it was, she brought the car to a halt outside the main entrance with a refined squeal of the brakes, raced up the stairs two at a time and skated to a halt in the bedroom at the sight of Rafe in the process of tucking a snow-white shirt into his waistband.

He slanted her a dark penetrating glance as he slid

the zip fastening home on impeccably-cut black trousers. 'You're late.'

'So—shoot me.' The flippant response covered an agitation caused by screaming sirens...police, ambulance, fire truck, an all too vivid imagination, and a painful reminder of her own father's accidental death in a similar situation.

His eyes narrowed. She looked faintly spooked, her eyes were a little too bright, not, he was sure, caused by flying up the staircase like a whirlwind.

He discarded the tie he was about to fasten, and closed the space between them. 'What's wrong?'

A week, and he could read her mind, divine her emotions? Surely she wasn't that transparent? 'I don't have time for an explanation.'

Rafe caught her chin between thumb and forefinger, tilting it so she had to look at him. 'A few minutes is neither here nor there.'

It was private, personal, and she didn't want to talk about it. 'Please, I need to shower, dress and be ready—' she paused briefly '—in twenty minutes.'

'Thirty will do.'

He didn't release her, and she threw him a fulminating glare. 'What is this? An inquisition?'

'I can easily find out,' he said quietly. 'So why not tell me?'

'Relentless bastard, aren't you?'

'The first is true, the second inaccurate.'

The glare intensified. 'You're driving me mad.'

He traced the pad of his thumb along her lower lip and felt it quiver beneath his touch. 'So what else is new?'

She held out for a few long seconds, then chose capitulation and relayed the reason for her delay.

'Something that revived the memory of how your father died.' The knowledge explained her agitation.

Fact, not a query, she noticed, and couldn't help wondering how closely he'd tracked the life of Joaquin d'Alboa's son and the lives of his widow and child.

'Go have your shower.'

Danielle escaped, managing to emerge twenty-five minutes later, dressed, her make-up complete, with her hair swept high into a knot atop her head.

The classic slim-fitting black gown with its spaghetti-thin straps showed her slender shoulders to advantage, accented the elegant slope of her neck, and showcased the gentle upper swell of her breasts.

She suffered Rafe's swift appraisal as she fixed on ear-studs, then she caught up her evening purse and preceded him from the room.

As dinner parties went, this had to be one of the more lavish, Danielle determined an hour later as she stood at Rafe's side sipping vintage champagne.

At least fifty guests assembled on a spacious terrace adjacent to colourfully lit gardens with manicured flower beds, topiary, decorative paths and seats placed at strategic intervals.

Uniformed waiters proffered trays containing a mix of canapés and savouries, and drinks.

'I neglected to ask,' Danielle ventured quietly. 'Is this merely social, or a function to aid a needy charity?'

'Ostensibly charity.'

'To which you've contributed a generous donation.'

Rafe inclined his head. 'I lend my support to a few worthy causes.'

He looked impressive attired in a dark evening suit that owed much to its Italian tailoring, for it fitted him like a superbly moulded glove, accenting an enviable breadth of shoulder, a lithe, muscular frame.

It made her think of what lay beneath the fine clothing, and it was no hardship at all to recall that toned body unadorned, the texture of his skin, the strength of muscle and sinew.

The image of his mouth angling in to capture her own, the feel of his hands on her body, skimming lightly over her skin, the intense sensual pleasure...

Stop it. The words were a silent scream. She suffered his lovemaking because it was part of the deal. Dammit, it was a major part of the deal, given conception was the ultimate aim.

A fellow male guest crossed to their side and, after an initial greeting, engaged Rafe in a business discussion.

Danielle welcomed the distraction, excused herself and moved towards a waiter with the intention of replenishing her drink...something definitely non-alcoholic this time out.

She caught snatches of meaningless conversation, and she had just selected a glass of chilled mineral water when she heard someone speak her name.

Turning, she summoned a polite smile and kept it in place. Cristina. Tall, elegant, exuding the patina of *class* bred from extreme wealth and exclusive private-school education.

'You must enjoy being active on the social scene again after such an—' there was an effective pause '—unfortunate absence.'

Careful, Danielle bade silently. Keep it polite and simple. 'Yes.'

Something shifted in Cristina's icy grey eyes. 'Interesting how you and your mother managed to effect such a reversal of fortunes.'

'Isn't it?'

'What did you do, darling? Sell yourself?'

This had the potential to become nasty. 'If that were true,' she managed evenly, 'why would marriage come into the equation?'

'Something that is on the tip of everyone's tongue.'

Danielle managed a slight smile, and refrained from comment.

'So, tell me,' Cristina pursued. 'Why *you*?'

'Perhaps you should ask Rafe?'

'You can't be *that* good in bed.'

She'd had enough. Polite conversation was one thing. Snide comments were something else. 'No?'

The blonde's gaze assumed a speculative gleam. 'Hope you can keep up with him, darling. He's a lusty son-of-a-bitch.'

'Mmm.' She aimed for a smile that was both dreamy and sultry. 'Isn't he, though?'

She'd gained an enemy. If she'd had any doubt, the sudden flash of jealous rage merely confirmed it.

'Just for the record,' Cristina stated with deliberate

calm, 'a wedding ring on a man's finger doesn't faze me at all.'

'And you'll be waiting to catch him if I fall from grace?'

'*When*, sweetheart. Rafe doesn't stay satisfied with one woman for long.'

'Well, now, maybe I'll be the exception.'

The raking appraisal bordered on the insolent. 'I very much doubt it.'

'What do you doubt, Cristina?' Rafe queried with a practised drawl.

He possessed the silent grace of a jungle cat, appearing at their side without warning.

The blonde recovered quickly. 'We were discussing La Femme, darling. Its relocation will prove to be an enormous success.'

She was good, Danielle conceded, and wondered if Rafe bought it.

'You'll excuse us?' He caught hold of Danielle's hand and threaded her fingers through his own, then he lifted her hand and brushed his mouth across her knuckles, eliciting a sharp glance.

'Damage control, Rafe?' She attempted to pull her hand free, and felt his fingers tighten. 'I can take care of myself.'

'Cristina has all the instincts of a piranha.'

'She has her sights on you.'

'My bank balance,' Rafe corrected drily.

Danielle cast him an analytical look, intrigued by his features in profile, the angles and planes reflected by lighting and shadows.

It was a strong face, the sweep of his jaw, the wide

forehead, symmetrically positioned nose, and a mouth to die for.

'Nice to know you have no illusions,' Danielle said sweetly.

He smiled, and her stomach executed a backward flip. It gave him an almost boyish look. Although she doubted he'd ever enjoyed boyhood. He'd gone straight from child to man, fashioned by the harsh law of human survival.

'You have a sassy mouth.'

'It's one of my talents,' she relayed solemnly.

'Our hostess is about to announce the buffet.'

A sumptuous array of food was set out on an extended table, and Danielle transferred a few morsels onto her plate. Bite-size portions and cutlery forks made for ease of eating, enabling the guests to move at will, converge with whoever they chose, lending a pleasant informality to the evening's proceedings.

Fund-raisers took various forms, Danielle mused, and success depended largely on the generosity and ingenuity of the charity organisers.

Tonight's effort followed a familiar pattern...ply the guests with drink, allow time to mingle, feed them, then while they're relaxed and mellow, provide the main event.

In this instance, the main event was an auction of memorabilia.

A set of Baccarat crystal goblets purported to have held Cristal champagne served at the table of visiting European royalty. A jade pendant worn by a past premier's wife at a function attended by an Arabian prince.

Danielle's attention was riveted by one item on display. The jeweller's box was distinctive, together with the exquisite diamond bracelet it held. Hand-crafted, the linking design was unique, and she recognised it as a bequest gifted to her four years ago on the advent of her twenty-first birthday. Retaining the matching earrings had been a sentimental act, but the bracelet had been sold off last year in one of many desperate bids to maintain a cash flow.

What was it doing here, and *who*...? No, he couldn't have. She shot Rafe a penetrating glance, and could determine nothing from his expression.

The auction began, and the bracelet was tabled as once belonging to a member of the Spanish aristocracy.

Rafe began the bidding, and Cristina's participation drew interest, causing the bidding to escalate as others joined in. Soon it reached an amount that saw the bid for ownership reduced to two. For every bid Cristina made, Rafe topped it, until an obscene figure was reached and Cristina declined to increase Rafe's bid.

Had it been Rafe's intention to make a public issue of Cristina's defeat? Most everyone present couldn't fail to miss the connection between his bid for the bracelet and its original ownership.

The list went on, and bidding was intense, culminating in a considerable sum raised for a charity specialising in providing terminally ill children with their dearest 'make-a-wish' fantasy. This evening's event would fund a return trip to Disneyland for a young leukaemia patient, her mother and a registered nurse.

Afterwards there was coffee, and the successful bidders paid for and claimed their purchases.

Rafe returned to her side, extracted the bracelet from its case and fastened it onto her wrist. 'Yours,' he declared quietly.

She ran the tip of her fingers over the precious stones. 'Thank you. It belonged to my paternal grandmother.'

He cast her a studied look. 'It was among jewellery acquired by my agent.'

Jewellery she and her mother had been forced to sell. 'You chose to donate something already owned, then buy it back? Why?'

'A whim, perhaps?'

Danielle doubted any action he took was motivated by something as frivolous as a *whim*. He was a superb strategist who calculated to win.

Guests began to disperse, and she joined Rafe in thanking their hosts, then walked at his side to the car.

It was a mild summer evening, the sky a dark indigo studded with stars, and there was a freshness in the air that boded well for a fine day tomorrow.

The drive home didn't take long, and as soon as Rafe garaged the car Danielle slid from the passenger seat and walked through to the lobby.

Thank heavens tomorrow was Sunday and she didn't need to race the clock or the traffic. She fancied a lazy day, preferably spent catching up with some accounting work on her laptop, maybe taking time to meet Ariane for a coffee.

She made her way upstairs to the bedroom, slid off

the stiletto heels, then reached for the zip fastening on her gown, only to discover Rafe's fingers about to complete the task.

With the zip freed, he slid the shoestring straps over each shoulder, then let the garment slip to the carpet.

As the gown was fully lined with an inbuilt support bra, all she wore beneath it was a pair of black thong briefs.

Danielle felt him slide the pins free from the elegant twist, and her hair fell to her shoulders.

Rafe turned her to face him, and she stood still, her eyes watchful as he shrugged off his jacket, then he discarded his tie and loosened the top few buttons on his shirt.

He cupped her face and angled his mouth over hers in a kiss that coaxed and seduced, then became intent on possession.

His hands shifted, one fisting her hair while the other slid down her back and cupped her buttocks, drawing her body in against him as he deepened the kiss to something that was almost primitive.

He was wearing too many clothes, and he dealt with them, then lifted her against him and parted her thighs so the most sensitive part of her was pressed to the hard bulge of his arousal.

The gentle sliding movement he initiated nearly drove her mad, and she groaned in encouragement as he tore off her briefs and tumbled them both down onto the bed.

He entered her in one long thrust, stilled, then took it slow and deep as she expanded to fit him. The rhythmic tightening of her inner muscles almost caused him to lose control, and he fought against it as he drove them both high onto a sensual plane where there was only the intense joy of fulfilment, the exquisite sensation of two people completely in tune.

Rafe supported his weight as he rested against her, nuzzling the sensitive hollow at the edge of her neck, then he trailed his lips to her breast to tease and provoke the burgeoning peak.

He felt her body quiver in response, and he absorbed her faint groan as his mouth settled over hers in a kiss that started sweet and slow, then built into something so incredibly erotic it was impossible not to be completely caught up with renewed desire.

In one fluid movement he rolled onto his back, and she arched against him, exulting in the sense of power as she took him on a ride that teased, tantalised and tested his control. The brush of her hair against his chest, the trail of her fingers as she explored the shape and texture of his body...enjoying the faint hiss of his breath, the husky growl low in his throat.

'Are you done?'

'Hmm, not yet.' She teased one male nipple with the edge of her teeth, nipped, then suckled, and took pleasure in his indrawn breath.

'When you're through playing, *querida*...'

Playing? She bit him, the fine edge of her teeth drawing blood, then she arched against him in a movement that was distinctly feline and rode him deep, increasing the pace until they met at the sensual pinnacle, held, then joined each other in a spiralling free-fall that left them both slick with sensual heat and gasping for breath.

Dear lord...there was almost a reverence apparent as she rested against him. Her body still pulsed in tune with her ragged breathing, and she felt the light touch of his hands as he skimmed the surface of her skin, soothing her until she gradually stilled.

Would it always be like this?

A woman could become addicted to the intense passion they'd just shared. Add *love*, and it would be a dynamic explosive mix.

As much as she'd vowed to hate him, her body was at variance with her brain, becoming a finely tuned instrument beneath his skilled touch. For that alone she wanted to hate him afresh. And herself, for her lack of control.

On the edge of sleep, she felt the brush of his lips against her forehead, and she sighed, too enervated to protest or to move.

CHAPTER SIX

DANIELLE woke alone, and she stretched, considered burrowing her head into the pillow for another hour, then opted against it.

The sun was shining, the whole day lay ahead, and she intended to devote part of it to updating La Femme's records, followed by some retail therapy.

It was ages since she'd been able to do any serious shopping, and, given her husband's social schedule, she needed to replace a pair of stilettos and acquire a new gown.

She slid from the bed, showered, pulled on jeans and a cotton top, tidied the bedroom, then ran lightly downstairs to the kitchen.

Danielle settled for cereal and fruit, followed it with toast, and made fresh coffee.

There was no sign of Rafe, and no note to provide an indication of where he might be. The study? The downstairs gym?

Danielle poured a second coffee, leafed through the Sunday papers, then she collected her laptop and briefcase, set both on the informal dining-room table and began to work.

It was there Rafe found her more than an hour later when he entered the kitchen after a punishing session in the gym.

'Good morning.'

She lifted her head, and felt her heart leap to a quickened beat at the sight of him in shorts, sweat-patched T-shirt and trainers. 'Hi.'

He crossed to the refrigerator and extracted a bottle of chilled water, broke the cap, and downed half the contents in one long swallow before turning towards her.

'I'll organise for one of the upstairs rooms to be furnished as a study for you.'

'That isn't necessary. I like the flexibility of being able to work anywhere. Keeping the records up to date rarely takes me more than a few hours each week.' At least it had up until now.

Rafe shot her a penetrating glance. 'It'll be easier if you have your own office space.'

Case closed. She knew she should be grateful. So why was there a niggling resentment apparent?

He drained the water bottle, dispensed with it, then walked from the kitchen.

An hour later Danielle closed down the laptop, gathered papers into her briefcase, then deposited both upstairs, checked her watch, then caught up her bag and car keys, and went in search of Rafe to let him know she'd be out for the rest of the day.

Except he was nowhere in plain sight, and she wrote him a note, propped it on the kitchen servery, then headed towards the garage.

Her first destination was Brighton, and she parked, then wandered at will, pausing at a trendy café for a cappuccino before browsing in the shops.

Her cellphone rang as she was about to enter a

boutique, and she retreated onto the pavement and took the call.

'Where are you?' Rafe's voice was unmistakable, and she mentally counted to three before answering.

'Precisely? Brighton, outside a dress shop.'

'Does the *not sure when I'll be back* in your note indicate late afternoon or evening?'

'Does it matter?'

'Answer the question, Danielle.'

'I didn't realise I required your permission to go out of the house.'

'*Querida.*' His voice was a dangerous purr. 'Don't test my patience, hmm?'

'Am I doing that?' she queried sweetly.

'Would you be so brave, I wonder, if you were facing me in person?'

'Count on it.'

His husky chuckle sent shivers scudding the length of her spine. 'Shall we begin again?'

She didn't pretend to misunderstand him. 'Evening. I want to call by the penthouse.'

'Six, Danielle. We'll take your mother to dinner.'

He ended the call, and she keyed in the digits to reach Ariane and relayed the invitation.

'Nonsense, darling. It'll be cosier if we eat here.'

Danielle wasn't sure *cosy* was a good idea. Her dear *mama* would doubtless indulge her romantic heart with a surreptitious analysis of the state of her daughter's marriage, despite or because of its circumstance.

'I'll make one of my specialities.'

It was so long since Ariane had been able to entertain. Resigned, Danielle queried, 'Is there anything you'd like me to pick up?'

'A fresh baguette from the bakery, darling. Oh, and some lettuce.'

'I'll come early and help with the preparations.'

'No, it'll give me pleasure to have you as my guest.'

Danielle ended the call, replaced the phone in her bag, then dedicated the next few hours to choosing a new gown and shoes.

It was after four when she let herself into the penthouse, armed with flowers, a bottle of wine, together with the baguette and lettuce.

A tantalising aroma permeated the kitchen, and she greeted her mother fondly, glimpsed the sparkling gleam evident in Ariane's eyes as she stirred the contents of various pots on the cook-top.

'For you,' she said with affection, gifting the wine and flowers, then she snagged a tea towel and fixed it at her waist. 'Now, what can I do?'

They worked happily together for the next hour, confident all was well, the serving dishes ready and the table set.

'Time to freshen up, I think,' Ariane declared.

The intercom buzzed, and Ariane released the external security door to allow Rafe into the building. Minutes later the chime bell sounded and Danielle added water glasses to the table setting while her mother let him into the apartment.

She heard their voices, his deep with its slight American accent, and sensed the pleasure in Ariane's greeting.

Danielle moved into the lounge, proffered a smile, and schooled her features as he crossed to her side, cupped her face and slanted his mouth over hers.

'What are you doing?'

'Kissing my wife.'

She wanted to slap him, and he knew, damn him! There was a humorous gleam evident in that dark gaze as he captured her mouth in a slow, sweet possession. A gesture that unnerved her, and brought pink colour to her cheeks.

It was a deliberate gesture, and one that would merely feed her mother's imagination. Which was precisely his intention.

'I thought we'd eat in,' Ariane declared. 'You'll be my first guests.' She sent her daughter a sparkling glance, then deferred to Rafe. 'What can I get you to drink? I have a nice chardonnay.'

The meal was a success, for her mother's culinary skills were notable, her delight in exercising them evident.

Cosy encapsulated the few hours they shared, and the developing rapport between Rafe and her mother was something Danielle viewed with caution.

There was a part of her that wanted to warn Ariane against a man who could manipulate circumstance at will. To advise Rafe's expressed affection was nothing more than an act, for it was laughable to contemplate otherwise.

His voiced interest in various framed photographs positioned on various items of furniture in the lounge sent Ariane delving into a drawer for more than one

family album, and Danielle deliberately absented herself on the pretext of making coffee.

She took her time, setting china onto a tray, adding
cheese and crackers to a plate, until the coffee had
filtered and there was no further reason for her to
delay a return to the lounge.

The fond hope the albums would be put to one side
weren't fulfilled, and she suffered through Ariane's
affectionate recount of foreign resort holidays and
various special-occasion photographs taken at different stages during her life.

It was too much information, acutely personal, and
left her feeling vulnerable.

'We must do this again,' Ariane enthused as Rafe
indicated they should leave.

'Indeed,' he agreed. 'As our guest. Danielle will let
you have the details.'

Danielle was silent as they rode the elevator down
to the basement car park, and Rafe walked to her car,
waited while she fired the engine, then followed in
his own vehicle.

They entered the driveway within seconds of each
other, and cut the ignition almost simultaneously.

Danielle gathered up the brightly emblazoned
carry-bags containing her purchases, then she entered
the foyer and made for the staircase.

'Your mother is a charming woman.'

'Yes, she is.'

Rafe followed her into the bedroom and began
loosening his tie. 'I'll ensure some of our invitations
include Ariane as a fellow guest.'

She deposited the carry-bags and stepped out of her

shoes. 'I know she'll appreciate that.' She slipped off her watch, removed the slender gold chain at her neck, and crossed to the *en suite*.

A leisurely shower, then bed. Tomorrow was another day, and there were a few items of stock due to arrive.

Danielle shed her clothes, turned on the water, then stepped into the shower stall. She picked up the soap and visualised the boutique window... She'd change the central mannequin's attire; maybe the black lace teddy—

The glass door slid open and Rafe stepped in. There was more than adequate room for two, but she resented him invading her personal space. Which was totally illogical, given the intimacy they shared.

'Must you?'

'You object?'

'Yes!'

He took the soap from her hand. 'Get used to it.'

'Look—'

'I'm looking, *querida*,' he drawled with amusement as he caught hold of her shoulders and turned her away from him. 'There was one photo in the album displaying a cute little birthmark.' His fingers trailed down her slender back to the curve of her buttock. 'Just about here. Ah, yes, there it is. How could I have missed it?'

Danielle wrenched out of his grasp, only to have him catch hold of her and turn her to face him.

Water cascaded against his back, and without thought she batted a hand against his shoulder, then clenched a fist and aimed it at his chest. 'Don't!'

His eyes stilled, the humour vanishing as if it was never there. 'You're treading dangerous ground.'

She raised stormy eyes to his. 'How would you feel if I began to examine *you* for any imperfections?'

'Aroused.'

'Of course,' she acceded with wicked cynicism. 'What else?'

'You want to make an issue of this?'

'Yes, dammit.'

'Why, when you have no hope of winning?'

'That doesn't stop me from trying!' What was the matter with her? To argue with him was madness. To do so when she was naked...insanity.

'What do you hope to achieve?'

She wrenched out of his grasp. 'If you don't mind, I'd prefer not to be used for sex tonight.'

Rafe pulled her back towards him and captured her head, tilting it so she had little option but to meet his gaze. 'And if I do mind?'

'You can go to hell.'

He was tempted to take her there. To show her the difference between taking and pleasuring. For a millisecond he almost did. Then he lowered his head and possessed her mouth, ravaging it in a manner that owed more to punishment than the desire to please.

He wanted her unbidden response, and he worked towards it, tormenting until he sensed her capitulation. Then he eased back, nipping the fullness of her lower lip with the edge of his teeth, teasing and provoking as she began to reciprocate, until the ardour was all hers and her hands lifted to link at the back of his neck.

In one swift movement he cupped her buttocks and raised her up against him, parting her thighs and plunging into her in one long thrust.

He watched her eyes dilate as she absorbed him, felt rather than heard her faint whimper at the suddenness of his invasion, sensed her body tense momentarily, then relax as he kissed her. Gently, with a sensitivity that made the breath catch in her throat.

Then he began to move, and she moved with him, caught up in the mesmeric passion of his possession. Helpless against a primitive hunger that changed her into a shameless wanton.

Danielle had no perception of time, and it seemed an age before she rested her head into the curve of his shoulder, totally spent.

Afterwards he moved beneath the water and cleansed her with a gentleness that almost made her want to weep, and she stood as he blotted the moisture from her skin before towelling himself dry.

On the edge of sleep she became vaguely aware that he caught hold of her hand and brought it to his lips.

The following few days were busy. Danielle effected a stunning window display that drew several compliments.

Business was brisk, although Wednesday proved to be a day where everything that could go wrong, did.

The courier failed to arrive as promised on the morning run, and the client sailed into the boutique prior to lunch expecting to collect her special order, only to become irate on discovering it wasn't there.

Apologies did little to appease, despite an assurance the order would certainly be included in the afternoon run.

It wasn't, and incurred a diatribe accusing La Femme of ineptitude, carelessness, together with promoting client dissatisfaction and a threat to take business elsewhere.

Danielle made a call to the supplier, and was informed they'd received a cancellation on that specific order, hence the reason why it hadn't been included.

A quick check with Ariane confirmed what Danielle already knew. Neither of them had initiated the cancellation. Leanne was excluded on the grounds she only worked on a Thursday, Friday and Saturday. The order had been faxed through on Monday, and today was Wednesday.

'Any ideas?'

Danielle gave her mother a thoughtful look. 'I could be wrong.'

'Sabotage?'

'I hate to think it might be a possibility.' Her teeth worried her lower lip, and her eyes hardened. 'From now on we confirm each order by electronic mail with a specially devised code known only to you, me, and the supplier.'

She picked up the phone and organised the arrangement.

Nevertheless, it perturbed her. The relocated La Femme was proving to be highly successful. The boutique provided a wide range of imported stock and the level of patronage was good.

If it was sabotage, then *who*?

Cristina? Did her vindictiveness extend this far? Danielle didn't like the way the mental maths added up. If Cristina was responsible she'd have to get irrefutable proof before she could take any action. Supposition and suspicion weren't sufficient evidence.

It preoccupied her during the drive home, adding an edginess to her demeanour. What she needed was some rigorous physical activity in order to expend excess nervous energy.

A workout in the downstairs gym, followed by several laps of the pool appealed, and she wasted little time exchanging her working clothes for a bikini, then she pulled on shorts and a T-shirt and sped lightly downstairs.

It was a spacious room, containing a bench-press, electronic treadmill, exercycle, punching bag and weights. There was a locked wall cabinet containing a variety of martial arts weaponry...at least one of which could be considered illegal. Unless he held a license.

'Admiring my collection?'

He had the tread of a cat, and she turned slowly to face him. He was dressed in sweat pants and T-shirt, and had a towel draped round his neck.

'You're a martial arts exponent?'

Rafe crossed towards her with a fluid grace not found in most men. 'Does that surprise you?'

Very little about him surprised her. 'No.' There was a quality to him she hadn't quite been able to pinpoint...the spiritual attunement of mind and body, the supreme discipline of each, and the acquired skill of using both as an art form.

He rested his gaze on her attire. 'You want to work out?'

'Punch something,' she amended succinctly.

He detected the edge to her voice and wondered at it. 'Care to tell me why?'

'Not particularly.'

He battened down his amusement. 'Want a pair of boxing gloves?'

Danielle cast him a dark glance. 'I'm serious.'

'That bad, hmm?' He was tempted to take the fine edge of her anger, turn it into passion, and enjoy the process.

Instead, he crossed to a set of built-in cupboards along one wall, extracted the gloves and returned to her side. 'Give me your hands.'

He taped them, then moved to the punching bag and held it still. 'Ever used one of these before?'

'No,' she denied, following him. 'But it'll do.'

'In place of *who*?'

She was silent for a few seconds. 'I'm not sure yet.'

Rafe offered a few basic instructions. 'Go for it.'

She did. Until he stopped her after a series of blows, and when he tore off the tape she crossed to the treadmill, set the controls at a medium speed and kept up the pace until she felt she'd had enough.

Rafe was within her peripheral vision, and she could only admire his fluid grace of movement as he completed a series of martial arts exercises. Control and discipline in practice form; lethal in combat.

Her energy spent, she left the gym and moved to the indoor pool.

It took only seconds to strip down to her bikini, and she took a running dive into the crystal-clear water.

Danielle lost count of the number of laps she stroked before a dark head surfaced close to her own, and Rafe matched his pace to her own.

It was a while before she called a halt and trod water at the far end of the pool.

'Had enough?'

'Yes.'

'Feel better?'

'Some.'

'Then let's get out of here, shower, and go eat.'

She levered herself onto the tiled edge, then got to her feet and reached for a towel. 'I'll cook.'

'We could dine out.'

'I do a great steak salad.' She caught hold of her hair and squeezed out the excess moisture. 'Elena has the makings in the refrigerator. Served with Turkish bread and hummus, it'll be divine. Trust me.'

It was. Eaten at the table positioned on the terrace, and accompanied by a superb cabernet sauvignon wine.

It was a peaceful scene, overlooking the landscaped lawns with their neat garden borders, the various flowering bushes and shrubbery.

Danielle had a sudden glimpse of what it would be like with children…there would a swing seat, a slide, and a variety of outdoor toys. A dog to love and provide fun and laughter, and indoors a cat to curl up on a few favoured chairs. And the nursery, with its cot, bed, bookshelves and toys. A rocking-horse, and a rocking-chair so she could sit with a child snuggled in her arms.

A child. The reason for this marriage.

Could she already be pregnant? It was a possibility, but, given her own calculations—most likely not.

How long would it take? A silent bubble of wry laughter rose and died in her throat. Given Rafe's dedication to propagating progeny…not very long at all.

'Ariane reports business continues to show a markedly increased turnover.'

Danielle took a sip of wine, then held the stemmed goblet in her hands. 'Yes.'

'You have reservations?'

He was quick. Too quick, she perceived as she caught his discerning look. Had Ariane relayed the mystery of the cancelled order and the resultant ire from their dissatisfied client? Should *she*?

There was a part of her that wanted to deal with it on her own. Surely it couldn't prove too difficult, even if Cristina had covered her tracks?

'No,' she ventured. The success of the boutique was vitally important. To Ariane, to herself. It was a matter of pride, and integrity.

'But?'

'Why do you imagine there is one?' She hadn't meant to sound so cynical, but Cristina and her trouble-making potential rankled.

Rafe leaned back in his chair and examined her

features. Something was bothering her, and he meant to find out what it was.

'We're attending a photographic exhibition on Friday evening at the Simpson Gallery.'

'Updating the coming week's social calendar?'

'Yes.'

'Oh, *joy*.'

'Don't be facetious.'

'Perhaps it's simply an aversion to being on display.'

'Given time, our union will become old news.'

He was right, but it didn't help much. Especially with the spectre of Cristina constantly looming in the background.

'Sunday we've been invited to join friends for a few hours in the afternoon. Volleyball on the beach, followed by a barbecue.'

'What if I have plans of my own?'

'We compromise.'

She'd ensure they did, just for the hell of it. 'How about taking in a movie at the cinema?'

'We'll be on the Gold Coast next week.'

'Excuse me...*we*?'

'I have business there,' Rafe relayed with marked patience.

'I can't leave the boutique.'

'Yes, you can. Leanne will work Thursday and Friday.'

She wanted to hit him, badly. 'I would have preferred you discuss it with me first.'

The sun was going down, fading the sky and dim-

ming the landscape beneath it. Soon everything would
be shrouded in varying shades of grey and pewter.

Remote sensors activated electric garden lights, illuminating the grounds in a soft glow.

Without a further word she rose to her feet and
began gathering up china and cutlery, then carried
them through to the kitchen. Within minutes she'd
restored order, and she ran lightly upstairs to retrieve
her keys and purse.

The need to escape, if only for an hour, was par-
amount.

'Going out?'

Danielle turned and saw Rafe framed in the bedroom doorway. 'Yes.'

'I'll get my jacket.'

Resentment flared, and lent her eyes a fiery sparkle.
'I'm going alone.'

His stance didn't alter. 'I go with you.' His voice
was pure silk. 'Or you don't go at all.'

Anger intensified as she threw him a furious look.
'I don't want to be around you right now.'

'Tough.'

'Dammit! You can't—'

'Yes, I can.'

'Why are you making this such a major deal?' she
demanded, sorely tried, watching warily as he moved
into the room.

'Because no woman of mine goes out into the night
alone.'

'I am not your *woman*.'

A faint smile curved the edge of his mouth. 'Yes,'
he acceded in an indolent drawl. 'You are.'

'Not in *any* sense.' She was so angry she could spit, and irked no end that he found it amusing.

He caught up a jacket, hooked it over one shoulder, then he slanted her a quizzical glance. 'Let's go.'

'I've changed my mind.'

'We could always have an early night.'

His implication was clear, and she clenched her hands in anger. 'Sex.' She threw him a fulminating look. 'Is that all you think about?'

'With you, it isn't a hardship.'

She acted on impulse and aimed a stinging slap…except it was intercepted before the palm of her hand could reach his cheek.

In seeming slow motion he tossed his jacket onto a chair, then he pulled her close and fastened his mouth on hers in a punishing kiss that reached right down to her soul as it invaded, plundered and conquered.

Danielle fought him at first, beating her fists against his ribs, his back, anywhere she could reach. Except it did no good at all, as he simply hauled her up against him.

His arousal was a potent force, and she struggled against him until her brain registered what her body had already accepted.

The need to respond was uppermost, and the knowledge caused a silent groan of despair as she attempted to wrench herself from his grasp.

She managed it, only because he released her, and she stepped back a pace as she fought to control her rapid breathing.

'Do we go, or stay?'

He sounded so cool, it merely heightened her anger, and she raised stormy eyes to his. '*I'm* going out. Alone.'

'We've already done that. You don't want to do it again.'

'You're not my jailor!' She moved past him, and quickly descended the stairs. Her car stood in the garage, and she used the remote modem to lift the automatic doors, then slid into the driver's seat and ignited the engine.

At that moment the passenger door opened and Rafe slipped into the front seat.

Rafe doubted she had any particular destination in mind, and he didn't offer a word as she cleared the gates, then headed towards the city.

Southbank suited her mood, for there were several cafés and coffee bars from which to choose, plus the pleasure of sitting outdoors and watching the world go by.

Maybe if she ignored Rafe she could pretend he wasn't there?

Fat chance, she concluded minutes later as she chose one café, selected an outdoor table, took a seat, and ordered a latte.

'A short black,' Rafe indicated, then sank back in the chair and subjected the woman opposite to an encompassing appraisal.

'Are we going to sit in silence, or attempt to communicate?'

Danielle met his gaze with equanimity. 'Pick a subject.'

'Whatever it is that's bothering you.'

'*You* bother me,' she retaliated. 'You make plans without consulting me, and expect me to conform.'

'For you to conform is part of the deal.'

'Of course.' Her eyes darkened. 'Let's not forget *the deal*.'

His expression didn't change, although his voice was a silky drawl. 'Careful, *querida*.'

The waiter delivered their coffee, and Danielle stirred in sugar, then took an appreciative sip.

'I don't want to leave Ariane with the total responsibility of La Femme.'

Her mother was more than capable, and in normal circumstances she'd have no hesitation in absenting herself for a few days. Except she had an instinctive feeling that Cristina was intent on causing mischief. The more she thought about it, the more she was convinced the leggy blonde was behind today's contretemps.

The concern was what else Cristina had planned.

'Two days isn't a lifetime.'

The fact he was right didn't help at all. 'You're not going to give in, are you?'

He added sugar and stirred the dark brew. 'No.'

Danielle looked at him, and saw the unrelenting resolve evident. A man no sensible person would choose as an enemy.

Without a further word she finished her coffee, then rose to her feet, extracted a note from her purse and had Rafe close his hand over hers.

'You take independence too far.' He summoned a waitress, handed her a note from his wallet, then followed Danielle out onto the boardwalk.

Attired in black trousers, a casual cotton shirt un-buttoned at the neck, he looked the antithesis of the high-powered corporate executive. Yet there was something about him that attracted a second glance.

The evening air was fresh, and there was a breeze teasing the length of her hair. A few stray tendrils brushed her cheek, and she tucked them behind an ear.

A wolf-whistle pierced the air, but she didn't even glance towards the admirer, unaware she was the tar-get of his appreciation. Nor did she see the chilling look Rafe threw in the man's direction.

Soon they turned and retraced their steps, and Danielle heard the laughter as they passed various ta-bles, the chatter as couples enjoyed a late meal.

They reached the car and she handed Rafe the keys before slipping into the passenger seat.

The drive home didn't take long, and inside she made for the stairs, uncaring whether he followed or not.

Minutes later she shed her clothes, slid into bed and snapped off the lamp. Sleep didn't come easily, and she lay awake in the darkness for what seemed an age before Rafe quietly entered the room.

She heard the faint rustle of clothes being removed, and had a vivid image of him discarding each gar-ment, that broad-shouldered frame, taut midriff, the flex of muscle and sinew, the satin-smooth olive skin.

Heat flooded her body, and the familiar ache deep within longed for his touch. Dear heaven, why did her body act independently from the dictates of her brain?

She didn't want him. *Liar.* There was a need to lose herself in the physical act, to experience again and again the primitive, magical sensuality he was able to arouse.

And just for a little while she wanted to be transported to that special place where it was possible to pretend what they shared was more than…just sex. Albeit very good sex.

For a moment the knowledge shocked her.

How could she even *think* her emotions could be involved? What was she…*crazy*?

She hated Rafe Valdez for the scheme he'd devised.

Except *hate* didn't form any part of what she felt as he reached for her. Dislike and apathy weren't even contenders as her body sang at his touch.

He had the skill, the knowledge to drive a woman wild, and as she went up in flames she didn't spare a thought for anything except the man, the moment, and the glorious, exhilarating ride.

CHAPTER SEVEN

DANIELLE couldn't help but wonder if Cristina had garnered an invitation to every function listed on the city's calendar for the social élite.

Coincidence or design? Given the glamorous blonde's intent to cause mayhem, it had to be the latter.

It was interesting to watch the society matrons work the gallery. A gracious word here, an overt hint there, and guests were rallied for the next event, be it social or a fund-raiser.

'Pensive thoughts?'

She turned towards Rafe and offered him a stunning smile. 'Observing.'

One eyebrow rose. 'Cristina?'

'However did you guess?'

'Any particular reason?'

She made a play at removing an imaginary speck from his immaculate jacket. 'She wants you. Can't you tell?'

'And that bothers you?'

'Why should it?'

Amusement lurked in that dark gaze, and a lazy smile curved the edges of his mouth. 'Let's examine the exhibits. The ones on the wall,' he added, placing a hand at her waist.

'You're killing me,' Danielle murmured. He had

no pretensions to grandeur, and merely played the role society expected of him. Whereas she'd been born into a class structure that lauded its peers, only to discard them when the chips began to fall.

The exhibits were many and varied. Harsh black and white, subtle shades of grey. An abstract collage that caused interest due to its demand for individual interpretation.

Breathtaking beauty vied with stark reality, and Danielle stood transfixed by the print of a child with cherubic features and eyes so incredibly sad their expression tugged her heartstrings.

She moved close, read the descriptive explanation printed beneath, and wanted to weep. A Bosnian child captured in a war-torn land, and deprived of family. Such innocence, so much grief.

Danielle felt a pulse thud at the edge of her throat. The thought of a child of her own suffering in any way almost killed her.

The fierce maternal instinct caught her unawares. It also endorsed the real reason for her marriage to Rafe Valdez.

She'd counted on her dislike of him. Putting up with sex as a means to an end. Playing a part in public, whilst leading separate lives in private.

Except it wasn't quite working out the way she'd envisaged.

No matter how hard she tried, it was becoming impossible with each passing day to distance her emotions, for he had only to touch her, and her pulse raced to a quickened beat.

It was all very well to abide by the adage *take each*

day as it comes...the days were fine. It was the nights—

'Rafe, darling.'

Danielle turned slightly at the sound of that husky feminine voice.

Cristina. Who else?

'I'd value your advice on a business proposition I'm considering.' The blonde offered Danielle a faint smile. 'You don't mind if I steal him for a few minutes?'

'Go ahead.' The proposition was undoubtedly a foil, but why should she care? Except she did, and that rankled more than she wanted to admit.

Fool, she derided silently. What possessed you to imagine you could become intimately involved with a man like Rafael Valdez, and keep your emotions intact?

Could he control *his* emotions?

Without doubt. The weak and undisciplined didn't survive the city streets. He'd acquired a sophisticated veneer during his rise and rise within the financial sector, and he fitted well into the social scene. However, the ruthlessness was evident beneath the surface, a heartless savagery that boded ill for any adversary.

For Rafe, she was the chosen vessel to conceive and carry his child, to provide essential maternal succour during its vulnerable early years. Once that had been achieved, it would be a case of mission accomplished, and she'd be released, financially taken care of as a salve to his conscience. Except men of Rafe's ilk didn't possess a conscience.

So, *get over it*, she chastised silently. Abide by the deal, and move on.

'Danielle. How nice to see you again.'

A familiar voice, and she turned with a ready smile. 'Lillian.'

'I'm endeavouring to organise something a little different as a fund-raiser. I thought possibly you and your dear mother might be interested in hosting a private showing of intimate apparel at La Femme. Invitation only, of course. We'd hire seating, provide the models, serve champagne and orange juice, bite-size appetizers. Included in the ticket price would be a voucher offering a ten per cent discount on items purchased at La Femme. What do you think?'

'I'd need to discuss it with Ariane,' Danielle said evenly. 'We'll also require detailed costing.'

'My dear, the costing isn't an issue. All I require from you is La Femme as the venue. The ten per cent discount will be your contribution.'

It was an attractive proposition, given the invited guests would undoubtedly spend, and spend well. 'What numbers are you considering?'

Lillian offered a triumphant smile. 'I thought fifty guests, seated in double rows of ten on each side, with two rows of five just inside the entrance.'

Naturally the boutique would need to be closed to the public during the showing. 'What time-frame are you looking at?'

'Two hours. Say, from two until four in the afternoon, tentatively mid-week, two weeks from now?'

'Put it in writing, Lillian, then I'll get back to you.'

'My dear, I already have.' She reached into her

bag, extracted an envelope and handed it to Danielle. 'Ring me tomorrow with your answer.'

Ariane would go for it, she was sure. It meant good business for La Femme, and profit was the name of the game.

Danielle moved between the exhibits, murmured an acknowledgement to a few people she knew, then paused in front of an enlarged print of a Harley Davidson motorbike. She couldn't decide who commanded more attention...the bike or the long-haired, black singlet-clad, heavily tattooed man who sat astride the seat.

'Some women's fantasy,' a familiar voice drawled, and she felt Rafe's touch at her waist.

'Hmm,' she agreed. 'All that pulsing power.'

'Are we talking about the bike here, or the man?'

She didn't miss a beat. 'Oh, the *man*. Bikes don't do it for me.'

'Image is everything?'

She cast him a studied look. 'You changed yours.'

'To fit the mould I shaped for myself?'

'Yet beneath the fine clothes, the practised sophistication, is the core of the person you were. That doesn't change.'

'So, in your opinion, I'm still a veteran of the Chicago streets.'

'You're Rafael Valdez,' she submitted solemnly. 'A man who fits easily into any background, and someone only the foolish would challenge.'

His eyes were impossibly dark, but humour lurked at the edge of his mouth. 'Is that a compliment?'

'A statement.'

He could shed his acquired image as easily as he'd assumed it. Become again what he had once been. It was there, something indefinable in his stance, the look of him. A waiting, watching quality, the hint of acutely attuned senses. In the name of survival, and protection of his own.

Did she come into that category? It was a thought she chose not to pursue.

'You spoke with Lillian?'

'Yes. She offered an interesting proposition.' She relayed it to him. 'What do you think?'

Progress, he acknowledged, aware that a week ago she wouldn't have mentioned it, let alone asked his opinion. 'Lillian has connections, and it will be a good advertisement for the boutique.'

It matched her own conclusions, and she was about to say so when she had the uncanny sensation she was being watched. With unhurried ease she turned slightly and became trapped in Cristina's gaze.

Venom glittered in unmasked brilliance for all of a few seconds, then it was gone, and Danielle suppressed a faint shiver. Such hatred!

'Can we leave?' She needed to get out of here, feel the fresh evening air on her face, and put as much distance as possible between her and the glamorous blonde.

If Rafe sensed the reason behind her request he gave no indication, and five minutes later she breathed a sigh of relief as the car eased out onto the main street and headed towards Toorak.

Numerous cafés were open, with patrons lingering over coffee at outdoor tables along the sidewalk. Rafe drew into the kerb and parked, and together they selected a table, ordered, then relaxed as they waited for their coffee to be served.

Rafe's cellphone pealed, and he took the call, spoke for a few minutes, then cut the connection.

'Business?'

'I need to access the computer, and email data through to New York.'

'Do you want to leave?'

'It can wait.'

He worked long hours and took minimum leisure time. Even then leisure connected with business. He could more than afford to cut some slack, delegate. Except he knew from experience that when you took an eye from the ball, the game suffered. Besides, he enjoyed the adrenalin rush of planning a deal and having it reach a satisfactory conclusion.

He'd come a long way in the past ten years. He'd acquired a reputation, wealth, social standing, and he possessed the trappings that went with them. Fine homes in different countries, a wife. Soon he would have a child. An heir of his own blood to inherit everything he'd worked for.

Danielle d'Alboa *Valdez*. A woman who didn't hide her dislike of him, and was honest enough to enjoy what he offered without artifice. It made a refreshing change.

How would she react, he wondered, if he relayed he'd deliberately tracked Ariane's financial decline and fall from social grace with marriage to her daughter in mind? That it hadn't been a simple deal, but a well thought-out and carefully orchestrated plan?

That, instead of a few months in the making, the deal had formed in his mind as long as a year ago?

She'd been right in accusing him of using her to his advantage. But not solely for her aristocratic connections. It was her pride and her courage that attracted him. And her honesty. For that alone he'd been prepared to pay the price. It was precisely those qualities he wanted in his child.

Rafe drank the strong dark brew and watched her with an indolence he knew she found unsettling.

She had the sweetest mouth, generously curved, and the delicate features of an angel. He felt himself harden at the mere thought of her unbidden response to his touch, and he shifted slightly in his chair.

It had been a while since he had felt the need for a woman the way he wanted her. How her flesh quivered when he kissed the curve at the base of her neck. The leap of her pulse when he held her, and the soft moan that escaped her throat when he suckled at her breast.

As for the moment he possessed her...it was like grasping hold of something incredible.

He drained his coffee, waited until she finished hers, then he pulled out a note and rose to his feet.

It took only a matter of minutes to reach home, and he resisted the urge to follow her upstairs. Work, he reminded as he crossed to the study and booted up his computer. An hour, two at the most, then he could join her in bed.

It was closer to three when he slid beneath the covers and gathered her close. He was fully aroused and needy, yet he took it slow until her response matched his own, and her unbridled passion became the sweetest gift as he led her towards ecstasy, then held her as they both went over the edge.

CHAPTER EIGHT

VOLLEYBALL, swimming, followed by a barbecue meant layered dressing, and Danielle donned a bikini, added a wrap-around skirt and matching top, then she tossed Lycra gym shorts and top into a gym bag, together with a towel, bra and briefs, minimum make-up and sunblock.

'Ready?'

'As ready as I'll ever be for a fun afternoon in the sun.' If Cristina happened to be among the guests, she'd scream.

Rafe added a towel to his gym bag, closed the zip, then led the way down to the garage.

He looked incredibly fit attired in fatigue-style shorts and a chambray shirt, his tall frame and breadth of shoulder emphasised by the casual attire.

He displayed an electric energy, a raw sensuality that made fools of women and reminded some men of their own inadequacies.

Dynamite. In the bedroom and out of it, Danielle accorded as Rafe brought the car to a smooth halt in the driveway leading to their hosts' stylish home.

Open-plan living, with an abundance of marble floors, modern furniture, and magnificent outdoor accoutrements, for there was a pool, a tennis court, and direct access to the beach.

Guests were already assembled on the spacious terrace, and she summoned a smile as she moved into their midst, greeting acquaintances. Women who had previously ignored her now gave the impression of being her very best friend.

It rankled, perhaps more than it should.

There were cool drinks, bite-size appetizers, and the ambience was casual. Designer gear was *de rigeur*.

'You're very quiet.'

She turned to the man at her side, and offered him a stunning smile. 'Forgive me, I didn't realise scintillating conversation was required.'

Rafe's eyes gleamed with musing cynicism. 'Our host will announce the volleyball event any time soon.'

'Thus providing the women an opportunity to cavort with the men, all in the name of sport.'

'*Cavort, querida*? I can think of a more pleasing way to expend physical energy than sport.'

Danielle directed him a level glance. 'I seem to recollect you did that last night.'

His soft, husky laughter almost undid her. 'Obviously I failed to make much impact.'

They both knew there was no truth to the statement. She'd reacted to his touch like a finely tuned instrument in the hands of a maestro. And barely restrained begging for more.

'I'm not into ego-stroking.' A flash of colour, the sound of tinkling laughter caused her to glance towards the French doors. 'I'll leave the lovely Cristina to make up for my loss.'

'Where do you think you're going?'

'Why, to mix and mingle,' she murmured. 'I don't intend to stay and watch her seduction technique.'

'You'd leave me to cope alone?'

Her mouth curved with wicked humour. 'Something you'll achieve with one hand tied behind your back,' she accorded, and turned towards the glamorous blonde. 'Cristina,' she acknowledged with pseudo-politeness. 'If you'll excuse me?'

'Of course, darling.'

Danielle wandered towards the bar and had her glass refilled with soda, then she glanced out across the bay, admiring the tranquil scene. Azure sky, blue ocean bearing colourful craft tacking across its surface. Cruisers, motorboats, families enjoying a weekend outing.

Inevitably her gaze skimmed back to Rafe, and she examined his features in profile. The strong jaw, the broad cheekbones, and well-groomed dark hair.

Cristina was intent on commanding his attention, and from here it looked as if the blonde was pulling out all the stops. The beautiful practised smile, the tilt of her head, the light touch of brilliantly lacquered nails against his forearm.

Charm personified, Danielle alluded, and dismissed the faint twinge of jealousy. To experience jealousy you had to care, and she didn't. So why did it irritate the hell out of her to see Cristina paw the man who'd paid for a child and several years of her life?

Almost as if he sensed her appraisal, he turned his head and slanted her a long, studied glance.

With a deliberate gesture, she took a long sip from

her glass then began an earnest discussion with the person standing close by.

It was perhaps as well their host chose that moment to announce the volleyball would commence.

What wicked wit had thought to place Cristina on the same side as Rafe and Danielle on the opposing side? Worse, the glamorous blonde had stripped down to a bikini. Grr!

This is the beach, Danielle silently chastised. Except fun was one thing; outright flaunting was something else.

Later, the players switched sides and Danielle found herself lined up next to Cristina. Not a good move, proven when she somehow managed to trip and land in the sand, orchestrated by a deliberately placed leg.

Well, two could play at that game. Except during the ensuing ten minutes she didn't get a chance to return an elbow jab or a stinging kick to a calf muscle.

It was a relief when the first round concluded and they retired to the pool while the remaining guests began their game.

Cristina executed a dive that showcased the perfection of her slender form. Danielle merely slid in from the pool's ledge.

She trod water as Rafe moved to her side. His eyes were dark, his gaze level, and she almost died as his mouth closed over hers in a kiss that tore the breath from her throat.

'What do you think you're doing?' she demanded the instant he lifted his head.

'Do I need a reason?'

'Yes.' With that she swam away from him, levered her body onto the side, then gathered up her towel, located her gym bag, and made for the guest pool-house.

It didn't take long to shower and change, and she emerged from the stall into the tiled lobby to discover Cristina waiting her turn.

'Pretty little scene you managed to engineer in the pool.'

This was getting tedious. 'I don't believe I owe you an explanation,' Danielle responded as she swept her hair into a careless knot atop her head.

'Watch your step,' Cristina warned, and Danielle met the blonde's gaze via mirrored reflection.

'All the time.'

'You don't stand a chance against me.'

She turned round to face a woman she knew to be her enemy. 'Be specific.'

'Figure it out, darling.'

'Are you threatening me?'

'You mean you need to ask?'

'Good luck, Cristina.' Her voice was a silky drawl, and she glimpsed a flash of rage before it was reined in.

'I never leave anything to chance.'

Danielle had had enough, and without a further word she effected a dignified exit.

The barbecue got under way around seven, with seafood kebabs, prawns, fish, and a variety of salads. Washed down with champagne it was a veritable feast.

The sun began to slip down beyond the horizon,

and dusk turned into dark. Electric lamps sprang to life, illuminating the terraced gardens and pool, and the sea became grey, almost black, as a silvery moon appeared in a star-studded velvet sky.

Coffee was served, and Danielle was conscious of Rafe's presence as they mingled among fellow guests.

It was after ten when the evening drew to a close, and she sat in silence as Rafe traversed the short distance home.

Indoors he re-set the alarm and followed her upstairs to their room.

'Nothing to say?' Rafe drawled as he began discarding his clothes.

'It was a pleasant afternoon, the food was great,' Danielle accorded matter of factly. 'Tomorrow's another day, I'm tired.' She shot him a piercing glance. 'Will that do?'

He crossed to her side, then hunkered down and examined her leg, pressing his fingers into her calf muscle.

'Must you?' she demanded, then winced at the sudden pain. 'That hurt.'

He massaged the muscle lightly, then unbent his length. 'You'll have a bruise.' His hand moved to her ribcage, and she slapped his forearm.

'Don't.' A useless directive, for he didn't take the slightest notice. 'Ouch.'

'I'll get some cream to reduce the bruising.'

'I don't need it.' She turned away from him, and stepped into the *en suite*. Within minutes she'd removed her clothes, donned a T-shirt, removed her make-up and brushed her teeth.

When she emerged into the bedroom he was standing beside the bed, tube in hand.

'Oh, for heaven's sake. Give it to me.' She went to take it from him, only to have him ignore her and apply the cream. 'Must you play nursemaid?' she vented angrily. 'Your ex-mistress is a vicious bitch.'

He finished with the cream, tossed the tube onto a nearby pedestal, then captured her face and lowered his mouth down to hers.

'That isn't going to work,' Danielle said the moment she could speak.

'I can see it won't.' He angled his mouth and took her deep.

When he lifted his head her eyes were glazed with passion, her lips pink and slightly swollen. He returned for more, grazing the curve of her mouth with the edge of his teeth before trailing to the edge of her neck and nuzzling there.

He sensed the silent groan in her throat, and caressed the vulnerable hollow where her pulse leapt to a quickened beat, then he pulled her gently down onto the bed.

Thursday morning they took a flight to Coolangatta Airport, then rode a taxi to the Palazzo Versace situated at Main Beach overlooking the broadwater.

The hotel itself was a drawcard for the tourists, and each of the privately owned condominiums provided a luxury only the wealthy could afford.

Italian in design, the mosaic tiles in the foyer were an art form, and Danielle gasped in sheer delight as she preceded Rafe into a luxurious condominium with views over the water.

Furnished completely by Versace-designed accoutrements, right down to cushions, china, cutlery, crystal.

It was, in a word, beautiful, and she told him so.

'Enjoy, *querida*,' Rafe bade indulgently. 'If you need to contact me, do so on my cellphone. I'll book dinner.'

It was a few years since she'd last visited the Coast, and she intended to explore. First priority was the apartment itself, the amenities, then she wandered into the adjacent Marina Mirage shopping complex, lingered in one of the cafés over a latte, and walked to Tedder Avenue at Main Beach, which had remained just as trendy as she remembered.

There was also the knowledge she wasn't pregnant, and she didn't know whether to be pleased or peeved at the discovery.

It was almost five when she entered the apartment, and she collected fresh underwear and headed straight for the shower.

Minutes later she gave a startled gasp as the door slid open and Rafe stepped into the tiled stall.

'Must you?' Danielle demanded fiercely.

'Why not relax and enjoy?'

'Forget seduction, it won't do you any good.'

They'd been intimate every night for almost three weeks. He didn't need for her to spell out the *why* of it.

His hands skimmed down over her shoulders and

rested on her breasts. 'There are many ways to indulge one another.'

'None of which I'm buying.'

A husky laugh left his throat an instant before his mouth captured hers, and the kiss left her wanting, needing more, much more.

It was a while before he lifted his head, and he traced the sensitive curve of her lip, his eyes as dark as her own.

'So be it.' He patted the firm cheek of her bottom. 'Now go.'

She did, and was almost dressed when he entered the bedroom. All she'd packed was a change of clothes and an elegant evening trouser suit in red silk. Black stilettos and matching evening bag completed the outfit, and she swept her hair into a smooth twist.

The restaurant overlooked the broadwater, and the food was to die for, so artistically arranged on the plate it was almost a sin to disturb it.

It was, Danielle decided, nice to be alone with him. No other guests at the table with whom she felt compelled to exchange polite conversation. And no possibility of Cristina intruding.

'Did you buy the condominium off the floor plan?'

'Two,' Rafe corrected imperturbably. 'One for my own use, and one to lease as an investment.'

Given the location and design, the value could only escalate.

'I gather your business meeting this afternoon was successful?' As if it would be otherwise.

'Yes.'

She lifted her glass and took a sip of wine. 'What time is our flight out tomorrow?'

'Late morning.'

Such a brief stay. Would they return in the not too distant future?

'Yes. In a few months,' Rafe drawled, and saw her surprise. 'You have expressive features.'

'Not so *you*.' It was impossible to read him, and she wondered if she ever would.

'Coffee?'

They took their time with it, then Rafe settled the bill, and they strolled along the boulevard, enjoying the night sounds. Luxury cruisers lay moored at the marina, and the numerous cafés lining the broadwater were busy with the boutique coffee crowd.

Rafe reached for her hand, and she linked her fingers through his.

Less than a month ago she'd sworn to hate this man, yet with each passing day there appeared a subtle shift in her emotions.

He was her husband, her lover. In time he would become the father of her child. Was it possible he could also be her friend?

And when their relationship was reduced to *friends*, how would she deal with it?

Not well, a tiny voice taunted. The knowledge slammed into her brain and settled there, sending her into contemplative silence.

Fool, she accorded silently. The wine has gone to your head. Rafe Valdez had presented her with a business proposition, which she'd accepted on his terms.

A business proposition their relationship would remain. Even if it killed her.

The days settled into a familiar pattern, and there was a sense of achievement as well as pleasure in seeing La Femme go from strength to strength with increased clientele and soaring profits.

At night Danielle dealt with the shimmering passion Rafe was able to evoke. Electrifying and incredibly sensual, it fed a primitive hunger and left her wanting more than just an enjoyment of the physical act.

Planning for Lillian's proposed fund-raiser took precedence as she conferred with Ariane and calculated the extra stock required, ensured the orders were placed in time for delivery.

The day duly arrived, and organisation was the key; that and lunch on the run, Danielle reflected as she closed the boutique, ensured the notice announcing a private showing was clearly visible, then she checked out the seating, adjusting a chair here and there to ensure they were staggered to enable guests seated in the rear row would be able to view the parade with ease.

A magnificent floral arrangement held centre place against the mirrored wall behind the counter...a *good luck* gift from Rafe.

'What do you think?'

'Darling, it looks wonderful,' Ariane enthused.

The caterers had not long delivered a variety of appetizers, and a large cooler out back held the champagne and orange juice.

The afternoon's programme had been rechecked twice, the lingerie and underwear set out in order.

Three models were due any minute, together with Lillian and a few volunteers to help out.

CDs were ready in the disc player, and it was just a matter of waiting for the guests to arrive.

At that moment Lillian breezed through the door with her volunteers, and two of the models followed close behind.

'There's a slight change of plan,' Lillian informed. 'The third girl we contacted to model has called in sick, and I've managed to find a replacement. It's so kind of Cristina to fill in at such short notice.'

At that moment the tall blonde entered the boutique and swept towards them.

Cristina? Saving the day, or employing subterfuge?

Danielle summoned a smile and subdued the desire to snarl. 'Kind,' she agreed, hating the role that forced her to be polite. 'The other models are in the fitting rooms. Leanne, our assistant, will go through the programme with you.'

Ariane checked her watch and moved with Lillian towards the entrance to greet the first group of guests.

By the appointed time all the chairs were filled, the champagne flowed, and the show was ready to begin.

So much thought and care had gone into its preparation, there was little chance of there being a hitch. Danielle had the programme memorised to the smallest detail, and the tension began to build as the first segment was shown.

After considerable deliberation, it had been decided to begin with sleepwear, then finish with the more daring thong briefs and minuscule bras. Three models, three colours in each category of styles.

La Femme now carried a full and varied stock of top French, German and Belgian labels guaranteed to please the most fastidious buyer.

Silk pyjamas in ivory, pale peach and cream drew murmurs of approval; exquisite full-length nightgowns and negligées were also a hit; the length changed with each round, until the most frivolous almost-there line was shown. Silk wraps in glorious colours followed.

So far, so good, Danielle breathed as there was a brief break while Lillian's volunteers refilled the guests' flutes with champagne and proffered appetizers.

'The feedback so far is excellent,' Ariane reported as they prepared for the next segment featuring slips in every length, colour and design, silk, satin, lace.

'Most everyone is marking items off on the programme,' Leanne informed. 'If they decide to buy you'll need to place a huge order for replacement stock.'

Dared she cross her fingers for luck? The temptation was almost irresistible.

The phone rang, and Ariane took the call, spoke a few words quietly, then she replaced the receiver and crossed to her daughter's side.

'Rafe, darling. He's in the area and will call in for a few minutes.'

A solitary man in a woman's domain? 'When?'

'He has just pulled up in the rear parking area.'

Danielle felt the tension headache accelerate. 'I'll

go let him in,' she managed calmly. Quite a feat when she felt anything but *calm* as she moved through the back room to unlock the door.

Rafe stood framed in the aperture, one hand casually thrust into a trouser pocket of his impeccably tailored business suit.

A dark angel, she accorded silently, and tamped down the slow-burning flame coursing through her body.

He shouldn't have this effect on her, and she assured herself she didn't covet it.

'What are you doing here?'

One eyebrow arched and his eyes assumed a humorous gleam. 'Is there a reason why I shouldn't be?'

Oh, hell, she had to marshal some control! 'It's unexpected.' She stood aside, then locked up behind him. 'The parade is in full swing.'

'It's going well?'

'I think so.'

Firm fingers caught hold of her chin and tilted it. *'But?'*

'Nothing.'

His gaze raked her features, caught the faint edge of pain evident, and brushed a thumb pad over her mouth. *'Nothing* gives you a headache?'

She managed to free herself from his grasp. 'Are you staying?'

He hadn't planned to. His original intention had been to move through the boutique, greet Ariane, Lillian, linger a few minutes to provide a little weight to the success of the parade, then leave.

Now he changed his mind. 'Will it disturb you if I do?'

Oh, my, what a question! 'I'm sure your appearance out front will *disturb* a few of the guests.' And delight one particular model.

His husky laughter sent warmth flooding through her veins. 'I'll try to be unobtrusive.'

'Sure, and pigs might fly,' she retaliated, and wasn't anywhere near quick enough to escape the brief hard kiss he bestowed on her mouth.

She shot him a dark glance as she reached into her bag, extracted a slim tube and took a few seconds to renew her lipstick.

Rafe's presence had just the effect Danielle anticipated, for the guests sat up a little straighter, smiled a little more brightly, and the models when they took the floor for the next segment seemed to possess a lighter step, their movements noticeably more provocative.

His eyes narrowed as he saw Cristina emerge, and his features remained expressionless as he observed the model's performance.

The blonde was trouble, and he had to wonder what lengths she'd gone to in order to replace the model contracted to appear at this afternoon's assignment. Somehow he doubted Lillian Stanich would have conspired to the change. It was more likely Cristina had enquired which models had been contracted, then offered one of them a higher fee to call in sick.

Exotic lacy teddies had little effect on his libido, although there was appreciation for the cut and style and the slender toned bodies of the girls who wore them.

He let his attention rest on his wife's features, and glimpsed the strain beneath her smile.

The parade was scheduled to conclude at four, and if he left immediately he'd still make his four-thirty appointment.

Danielle did her best to ignore him. Not an easy task when her mouth still tingled from his kiss, and she was battling with a mixture of resignation and anger at his presence.

Why didn't he go? Or was he deriving vicarious pleasure from watching near-naked young women parade in titillating underwear?

Satin bra and pants sets, briefs that ranged from hipster, bikini, to thong. The latter so minuscule the garment was a mere whisper of lace.

Cristina was in her element playing the role of seductive temptress as she circled the boutique, pausing every few steps to pose. Her gaze deliberately sought Rafe, and the tantalising sweep of her eyelashes, the soft pouting mouth, the witching smile all conspired to give the impression she was bent on reminding him what was on offer.

Danielle failed to see how anyone in the room could miss the blonde's blatant invitation.

The final segment concluded, Ariane relayed a gracious few words in thanks to Lillian for arranging the afternoon's gathering, and encouraged the guests to utilise their discount vouchers in aid of a worthwhile fund-raiser.

Coffee was served, together with petit fours, and

Rafe lingered only long enough to speak with Lillian, then he took his leave. But not before Cristina way-laid him on some nefarious pretext.

Danielle deliberately focused her attention on the guests lining up at the counter with their programmes and their discount vouchers.

Business was brisk. In fact, it was so good, a number of guests were still lingering in the boutique when it came to closing time.

Lillian, an exemplary organiser, had arranged for the hire firm to collect the chairs at five, together with the cooler, and after the final guest had departed Ariane, Leanne and Danielle began cleaning up and restoring order.

Consequently it was almost seven when Danielle entered the house, and she made for the stairs.

Rafe's car was in the garage, so obviously he was home. Hopefully he'd already eaten and was en-sconced in the study.

She reached the bedroom and entered the *en suite*, intent on filling the spa-bath, then she discarded her clothes, pinned up her hair, and sank into the warm water.

Bliss, she accorded silently as she switched on the jets, then she leant her head back and closed her eyes.

Danielle lost count of time as she reflected on the successful afternoon in terms of stock exposure and sales. The only fly in the ointment had been Cristina.

'That bad, hmm?'

Her lashes swept upwards at the sound of Rafe's voice, and her eyes widened as he hunkered down and handed her a flute of champagne.

He touched the rim of his flute to hers. 'To a successful afternoon.'

He looked vaguely piratical in dark jeans, his shirt unbuttoned and the sleeves turned back. This close he was a threat to her equilibrium.

'I forgot to thank you for the floral display,' Danielle offered politely.

'My pleasure.'

'It was thoughtful of you to stop by.'

He smiled, at least one step ahead of her. 'But a severe case of overkill to have stayed for more than an hour, hmm?'

She swept him a killer glance. 'The guests positively *glowed* in your presence.'

'My sole interest was one of support.'

'Really?' She wanted to throw something at him. 'That's why you stayed? Forgive me for imagining it was just to leer at the semi-nude models.'

His husky laughter was the living end.

'*Querida*, I was far more tempted just looking at you, knowing what lay beneath that chic business suit, aware that it's mine for the taking,' Rafe drawled, 'than viewing exotic underwear on women who have no appeal for me whatsoever.'

'Cristina didn't seem to think so,' she shot back.

'Naturally, as an exhibitionist with an impossible ego.'

'As far as she was concerned, she was giving a private showing just for *you*.'

'Jealous?'

She picked up the sponge and threw it at him.

He fielded it easily, tossed it back into the spa, then

he uncurled his lengthy frame. 'You want I should join you?'

'If you get in, I'll get out,' she offered succinctly, and felt her eyes widen as he pulled off his shirt and reached for the snap fastening on his jeans.

'I wouldn't bank on it.'

Danielle scrambled to her feet as he discarded his jeans, briefs, toed off his trainers, and he grasped hold of her arm as she attempted to step out of the tub.

'Let me go!'

There was something almost pagan about him as he joined her, a raw sexual energy that was infinitely primitive.

'Don't.' She tried to evade him, and found herself pulled down into the cradle of his arms.

'Relax.'

How could she *relax*, for heaven's sake?

Even as she struggled, his hands slid up her arms and he began kneading the tight muscles at the base of her nape.

Oh, God, that felt good. So good, she breathed silently, giving in to the magic of his touch.

After a few minutes she couldn't help herself. 'You do that very well.'

She felt the brush of his lips against the curve of her shoulder.

'One hopes it's not the only thing I do well.'

She could hear the amusement evident in his voice, and her body began to throb as sensation swirled, reaching every nerve-end until she felt as if she was on fire.

'What do you want? A score on a rating from one to ten?'

Laughter rumbled from his throat. 'Heaven forbid.'

'I'd like to get out now.'

'We're not nearly done.'

His hands left her shoulders and slipped to cup each breast, stroking the firm contours, then exploring each burgeoning peak.

The tactile touch ignited a flame deep within, and she groaned as his hand slid down over her stomach to the apex between her thighs.

All it took was a circling sweep and sensation spiralled, taking her high. His lips caressed her nape, and she arched against the sensual probe of his fingers. She cried out as he stroked the sensitive clitoris, convulsing at the intense oral stimulation, and she made no protest as he scooped her into his arms and stepped out of the spa.

Rafe snagged a towel and blotted the excess moisture from her skin, then dragged the towel over his body before leading her to the bed.

One tug and the bedcovers slithered onto the floor, then he pulled her down with him, entering her in one deep thrust.

It was she who began to move, she who dictated the pace, and she exulted in the power a woman could have over a man. Aware of the animalistic passion, and raw intensity that consumed them both as they climaxed, then tumbled in a glorious drift of sensual emotion.

Afterwards she slept, and it was almost midnight when they ventured downstairs to replenish their energy levels with something as prosaic as food.

CHAPTER NINE

SHARING breakfast on the terrace was a relaxing way to kick-start the day, and Danielle took a generous sip of strong coffee as she let her gaze wander over the gardens. Antonio's efforts with the lawns, the plants, showed tremendous care and dedication, and the visual effect was stunning. The couple's work hours coincided with her own, which meant they entered the house after she left and were gone by the time she returned.

Toorak was a well-established moneyed suburb, with a pleasing mix of modern and old homes, some of which stood in spacious grounds.

Rafe's home was no exception, and high walls lent an air of privacy and seclusion, despite the suburb's close proximity to the inner city.

'I have a week of meetings in Paris and London,' Rafe informed as he drained the last of his coffee. 'We fly out tomorrow.'

The *we* rankled. 'I suppose you've already discussed this with Ariane, Leanne is prepared to work, and the whole thing is a *fait accompli*.'

Rafe inclined his head. 'Would you have preferred a time-wasting argument?'

'You won't give me the option to refuse?'

There was an edge of humour apparent. 'Do you want to?'

She opened her mouth, then closed it again. *Paris*. She'd have the opportunity to visit the lingerie houses, revisit a few of her favourite places... A winsome smile curved her lips. 'Who would protest about a trip to Paris?'

Even in the cold, drizzling weather of a northern hemispheric winter, Paris still retained its magic.

Danielle dismissed the misty fog hanging heavily on the air, buttoned her coat and swung the woollen scarf round her neck.

It had been five years since she last visited, and there were places she wanted to explore, an art gallery, the Left Bank, a favoured café she'd haunted during her sojourn in this beautiful city.

The skies might be grey, but her mood was as bright as a rainbow.

She adored the ambience, the sense of history apparent. A place where battles had been fought long before, the generations of Parisians who'd walked these streets, the architecture...

It didn't matter that Rafe would be tied up in business meetings all day. There was the Louvre, Notre-Dame, and no visit to Paris was complete without viewing the city from the Eiffel Tower. St-Germain-des-Prés...

Danielle sighed, and quickened her footsteps, intent to make the most of the few days she had here.

There was the thrill of being able to shop, and, although she could have gone crazy with Rafe's credit card, she resisted the temptation by being selective. Very selective. A gift for Ariane, something small for Leanne, and a token for Elena.

It was after six when she entered their luxury hotel on the Avenue des Champs-Elysées and took the lift up to their suite.

Rafe was already there, his jacket discarded and his tie pulled free as he poured himself a drink.

He took one look at her pink cheeks and sparkling eyes, then he crossed the room and took her mouth in a lingering kiss.

'Good day?'

'Wonderful.' She offered him a smile that curled round his heart and tugged a little. 'You?'

'The French like to haggle.'

'A stand-off, huh?'

'You could say that.'

'And you won't give in.' It was a statement, not a query.

'No.' The deal, if it was cut, would be on his terms.

Danielle deposited the signature carry-bags onto a chair, and began unbuttoning her coat.

Rafe slid his hands inside its warmth and pulled her close to nuzzle the sweet hollow beneath her earlobe. 'Come share my shower.' His palms slipped low to cup her bottom, drawing her in against his arousal.

He wanted her, needing the sweetness, and more than anything he wanted to lose himself inside her, to hold her close and temporarily forget the frustrations of the day.

Then, he determined, they'd dress and go somewhere for dinner, eat fine food, drink a little wine, then stroll back to the hotel.

'I'm not sure that's a good idea.'

His lips brushed the edge of her jaw and settled on the edge of her mouth. 'No?'

'We might not get out of this suite.'

'And that's a problem?' He nipped the soft fullness of her lip, then soothed it with his tongue.

'This is *Paris*,' Danielle said simply, as if that said it all, and he chuckled an instant before he conducted a slow sweep of her mouth.

She kissed him back, and couldn't help the way her body responded as he deepened the kiss with a hunger that matched her own.

Their clothes were an impossible barrier, and they dispensed with them, letting them drop where they stood.

Rafe took a few seconds to throw back the bed-covers, then he tumbled her down onto the bed. He buried his mouth in the valley between her breasts, then tantalised each peak, rolling the tender nipple with his teeth in an action that held her on the brink between pleasure and pain.

Danielle arched up against him, circled one male aureole with her tongue, savoured it, then she nipped the hard pebbled nub...and felt his sharp indrawn breath.

Emboldened, she reached for him, tracing the satin-smooth skin sheathing his male shaft with a feather-light touch before sliding low to cup him.

His husky growl urged her to tease and tantalise, before conducting an erotic circling movement that had every muscle tensing in his body.

'Careful, *querida*,' he warned softly, and lowered his mouth to hers in an oral imitation of the sexual act itself. Then he entered her with one powerful thrust that took him to the hilt.

The feeling of enclosure was acute, given his sheer size, and he rocked a little, easing the pressure as her muscles caught his rhythm.

She hadn't thought it possible to feel like this every time, and she held on in a mutual slaking of desire that swept them high.

Was that her voice crying out? Begging? The thought fled as she became caught up in such a tide of emotion that she shattered into a thousand pieces at the moment of climax.

Dear heaven.

There wasn't a single word she could utter as he disengaged, then scooped her into his arms and carried her through to the *en suite*.

Cataclysmic whispered through her brain long minutes later as they soaped each other. Earth-shattering sex, she added silently.

Half an hour later they emerged from the hotel and walked briskly in the cold night air. They could, probably should, have frequented one of the hotel's restaurants, and not ventured outdoors.

However, fine restaurants lined the streets and avenues radiating off the Champs-Elysées, and they didn't need to walk far before they ventured into an élite establishment, where Rafe requested, in faultless French, the *maître d'* find them a table.

The wine, the food, both were superb; a true gourmet delight, Danielle complimented as she declined dessert and requested coffee.

Rafe had the look of a satisfied cat...a sleek panther, she decided, all too aware of the power beneath the Italian tailoring, the crisp white shirt.

Even thinking what he could do to her set all her nerve-ends on edge, and renewed warmth invaded her body.

He knew. She could tell from the indolent gleam in those dark eyes, the warm curve of his mouth.

'Danielle? *Danielle* d'Alboa?'

The voice was familiar, the man's features even more so.

'Jean-Claude?' There was disbelief in her voice, then soft laughter emerged from her throat as she lifted her face to receive his salutary kiss to each cheek. Her eyes sparkled. 'I don't believe it.'

'It is I who does not believe you are back in Paris, *chérie*.' He glanced from her to Rafe, and back again. 'Are you not going to introduce us?'

'Of course. Jean-Claude Sebert, Rafael Valdez.'

'Her husband,' Rafe drawled, intent on claiming ownership.

Danielle sensed the faint warning edge in his tone, and briefly wondered at it.

'Jean-Claude is an old friend,' she explained. It had been *years*, at least five, and he'd been very good to her. 'Please, you must join us. We were just about to order coffee.'

'*Chérie*, you are sure I am not intruding?' He glanced towards the man who had put a ring on her finger, and wondered at the wisdom of annoying him.

Rafe gestured towards the vacant chair. 'Please.'

'So, tell me, Rafael, how you managed to capture this delightful creature.'

'By presenting her with an offer she couldn't refuse.'

'I see.'

'I hope you do, my friend,' Rafe drawled, and, lifting a hand, he signalled the waiter to bring coffee.

'It seems so long since I last saw you,' Jean-Claude declared. His shoulders lifted in a Gallic shrug. 'Yet not so long.' His mouth curved into a warm smile. 'You are even more beautiful now than you were then.'

A mischievous smile widened her lips. 'And you are even more the flatterer, *oui*?'

'Ah, you know me well.'

'Jean-Claude was an art student at the Sorbonne,' she relayed, aware of Rafe's watchful gaze. 'We met whilst taking a tour of the Louvre. He was determined to set the world on fire with his art.'

'And have you?' Rafe queried with deceptive indolence.

'Not the world. Just a small part of it.'

'How small, Jean-Claude?' Danielle teased. 'You always were incredibly modest.'

'My work hangs in some of the galleries.'

Coffee was delivered by a waiter, and served. Danielle added cream and sugar to hers, while both men took theirs black.

'How long are you staying?'

'Only a few days,' Rafe informed, and saw the other man's disappointment.

'Tell me how things are with you. Have you married?'

'Briefly. It didn't work out,' he relayed with an eloquent shrug. 'Now I bury myself in my work.'

'I'm sorry.'

'Yes, I do believe you are.' He sipped his coffee, finished it, then rose to his feet and withdrew a note which he placed on the table.

Rafe waved it aside, but the Frenchman didn't pick it up.

'If you'll excuse me?' He brushed his fingers to her cheek. *'Au revoir, chérie.'* He turned to her husband. 'Rafael.'

She watched as he disappeared out onto the pavement, then she picked up her cup and sipped its contents.

'No, he wasn't,' she offered quietly, challenging Rafe's level gaze.

He didn't pretend to misunderstand. 'Did you love him?'

'He was there for me when I needed him to be,' Danielle said quietly. 'After someone I thought I loved proved to be more interested in the d'Alboa heritage than he was in me.' Her eyes were clear, with just the merest shadow of remembered pain. 'Jean-Claude picked up the emotional pieces and helped me put them back together again.'

And fell in love with her, Rafe added silently, wondering if she'd known.

'It appears I may have misjudged him.'

'For which you won't have the opportunity to make amends.'

'You didn't maintain contact?'

'It wouldn't have been fair,' she qualified simply.

Rafe summoned the waiter, and paid the bill. 'Shall we leave?'

They walked a while, pausing every now and then to peruse the shop window-dressing. The night was alive, with people seated in numerous cafés, the aroma of food and strong coffee redolent on the evening air.

There was a sense of timelessness, a vibrancy she hadn't experienced in any other major city in the world. Perhaps she was just viewing it with new eyes, but it seemed different.

Or maybe it was *she* who had changed. Fashioned by circumstance and the loss of a lifestyle she'd taken for granted. The realisation that dignity and integrity were more important than possessions and false friends.

It was late when they returned to their hotel suite, and Rafe crossed to the desk, opened his laptop, then set to work. 'I'll be a while.'

'Fine.' She'd slip into bed, and hopefully be asleep when he joined her.

She was, and an hour later he stood looking down at her features in repose, aware of the inner beauty of her soul. It tugged at him, awakening something deep within.

The following few days passed much too quickly, for there wasn't sufficient time to fit everything in.

Rediscovering the city was a wonderfully exhilarating experience as Danielle became reacquainted with the familiar and enchanted by the new.

It would have been fantastic to be able to take a

month instead of three days to explore. However, she managed to seek out two élite lingerie boutiques and elicit a preview of the new season's styles.

There was too much to see and do to linger long in any one of the many trendy cafés lining the boulevards and avenues, and she returned to the hotel each evening in time to shower, change, dine, then explore the city by night with Rafe in attendance.

All too soon they boarded a flight to London, and spent two days and a night there before returning home.

The telephone pealed, and Danielle crossed from the mannequin she was dressing to the counter to take the call. Ariane was engaged in the fitting room with a client.

'Good afternoon. La Femme. Danielle,' she intoned pleasantly.

'Have you received my replacement brief?' a feminine voice demanded with autocratic arrogance on identifying herself.

The client from hell. 'I was able to purchase the same colour, style and size whilst in Paris. It's here for you to collect at your convenience.'

There was a faint pause as the woman digested the information. 'I'll be in tomorrow.'

Great, Danielle perceived with a slight grimace. The woman seemed bent on causing trouble, returning a pair of briefs she'd purchased at the lingerie showing, insisting a small slit in the lace had been there at the time of purchase. Something both Ariane and Danielle knew not to be true, for each garment underwent a rigid check on delivery, and wasn't added to the stock shelves without inspection.

Which meant the slit had occurred after purchase. Whether it had been deliberate action or the result of an accident was debatable.

A lengthy and very vocal diatribe about careless workmanship, an accusation La Femme was selling falsely labelled goods at highly inflated prices indicated a deliberate attempt to denigrate.

Hence, Danielle had kept the receipt and packaging as proof.

It disturbed her, and made for extra caution. If the client had been Cristina the motive would be clear. But both complaints in the past ten days had come from different women.

It was something of a relief when several days went by with no mix-up with any special order, no one returned a supposedly flawed garment or lodged a complaint.

The boutique thrived, the catalogue went out, and on a social level it proved to be a very quiet week.

'Would you mind if I invite Ariane to dinner?' Danielle queried over breakfast Friday morning, and incurred Rafe's measured glance.

He had the power to render her helpless with just a look, and she wondered how he could sit there so calmly when only hours before they'd shared earth-shattering sex. Dammit, she could still *feel* the power of his possession, the acutely sensitised erogenous zones he was able to play with such innate mastery.

'Tonight?'

Get a grip. A silent admonishment that was of no help at all!

'I thought Sunday, unless you have plans.' She bit into the last morsel of toast, then followed it down with coffee.

'Sunday's fine.'

'I'll cook.' She wrinkled her nose at his faintly raised eyebrow. 'You doubt I can?'

'Did I imply otherwise?'

Just for that, she'd plan something incredibly exotic!

Rafe drained his coffee and rose to his feet. 'Don't wait dinner.'

'I won't be home. It's late-trading night,' she reminded, and followed him from the room, snagged her jacket, briefcase, then trailed him to the garage.

'Mmm,' Rafe murmured appreciatively as he entered the kitchen late Sunday afternoon. 'Something smells good.'

She looked cute in cut-off denim shorts and a singlet top. Her hair was caught into a pony-tail, she wasn't wearing a skerrick of make-up, and she had a smear of flour on one cheek.

He moved in and caught her close, only to have her slap his forearm. An action which had no effect at all as he leant down and fastened his mouth on hers.

When he lifted his head he took satisfaction in her slightly glazed look, although she recovered much too quickly for his liking.

'If you're going to stay in the kitchen you can be

useful.' She indicated a stack of pots and pans. 'You want to wash or dry?'

He'd served his time in a few restaurant kitchens in exchange for food. 'Go freshen up.'

She didn't need second bidding, and when she returned ten minutes later the kitchen had been restored to its sparkling best.

Ariane arrived at five, presented Rafe with a bottle of chilled wine, and laughingly spread her hands when Danielle refused her help.

It was a fine meal, and well worth the effort. Afterwards they took their coffee out on the terrace.

The air was fresh, the sky a deep indigo with a sprinkling of stars, and Danielle was loath to admit it had been a long time since she'd felt so relaxed.

CHAPTER TEN

'ARE you sure you don't mind if I leave early?' Ariane queried with an air of concern.

'Mid-week, and five o'clock?' Danielle queried with a smile. 'The boutique isn't going to suddenly experience a rush of clients. Now *go*. I can handle closing up.'

Twenty-five minutes later Danielle checked her watch and switched off the deck with its selection of CDs chosen for subtle background music. In a few minutes she could lock the front door, retrieve the cash float, then close up and leave.

The heat of the day would hit as soon as she exited the boutique's air-conditioned interior, and she conjured up an image of Rafe's pool, its cool, silky water. The thought of indulging in a few leisurely laps appealed before she showered and changed to attend a sculpture exhibition. An invitation-only affair, it was a private showing for a select coterie of proven clients and collectors of the sculptor's works.

Her mind strayed to the contents of her wardrobe. Black always made a statement, but perhaps—

The sound of the electronic door-buzzer surprised her, for it was rare for anyone to enter the boutique at this hour.

The young man's motorcycle gear and helmet

shouldn't provide any reason for her sudden instinctive spurt of alarm.

'Is there anything in particular I can help you with?' Danielle queried as she moved towards him.

Maybe he was here on behalf of a girlfriend, and had size, colour, style memorised or written down.

He indicated a mannequin to his left. 'Do you have that in black in a size ten?'

It took only a minute to open the appropriate drawer and extract the briefs. She double-checked the size tab, then crossed to the counter for tissue and ribbon, the carry-bag that was their trademark packaging.

Hard hands caught hold of her arms, and she cried out in shock as they were wrenched behind her back.

'What the hell are you doing?'

'Shut up.'

The motive had to be robbery, but she was damned if she'd accept it without a fight.

Quick reflexive action with the heel of her shoe found purchase, and she heard a grunt as she was pushed down onto the floor.

She struggled in vain, hating the ease with which he held her down. He had her hands in a crushing grip, and she was half-sitting, half-kneeling on the floor.

She didn't even think, just aimed her head at his leg and sank her teeth into a trouser-clad thigh.

Then she screamed in agony as fingers caught hold of her hair, wrenching her head back, and a resounding slap cracked against the side of her face.

'Bitch.'

Danielle's eyes watered with the force of the blow. 'Take the money and go.'

She heard the sound of masking tape being torn from its roll, followed by a harsh snort of derision, and she fought like a tiger before her captor successfully bound her wrists together.

Her hair, once caught into a sleek twist, now tumbled loose, and her breathing came in ragged gasps from her exertions.

He pushed his face close to hers. 'Try that again, and you'll wish you were dead.'

The look she cast him held a mix of disdain and fury.

'Nothing to say?' he taunted. His eyes were cold, cruel. With deliberate movements he reached out a hand and cupped her jaw.

'Don't...*touch* me!' Her anger was very real.

His smile held an evil calm. 'Try to stop me.'

She kicked out at him in a last-ditch attempt to harm as he grabbed hold of her legs. Masking tape at her ankles, then her knees made any further movement impossible, and she swore at him.

She watched as he opened the cash register, stuffed notes and coins into his pocket, then leant down and caught her chin in a punishing grip.

'By the time you get help I'll be long gone.'

He swept the briefs off the counter onto the floor, then disappeared out the door.

Danielle wriggled out of her shoes, then inched her way towards the phone. Dammit, who would have thought masking tape could be so effective?

If she could open a drawer and somehow retrieve the scissors, she might be able to cut herself free.

It took time, but she managed it. First her ankles, then her legs, her thighs. Once the scissors slipped, leaving a nasty scratch.

At least she could get to her feet and reach the phone. Dialling wasn't easy, and she punched in a wrong number, then had to start over.

Rafe picked up on the third ring. 'Valdez.'

'Someone has just robbed the boutique,' she relayed calmly. 'I need to file a police report.'

She heard him swear. 'Are you OK?'

Shaken, angry, but not hurt. 'Yes.'

'I'm on my way.'

He was there in five minutes.

Minutes during which she managed to wrestle with the scissors and slice through the tape binding her wrists.

He took in the scene at a glance, his features a chilling mask as he crossed to her side.

His eyes were impossibly dark as he caught the reddened patch marking her cheek. 'He hurt you.'

'It could have been worse.'

Rafe cupped her face. He brushed his fingers gently over her cheeks, then leant down and kissed her. A soft open-mouthed gesture that almost fractured her into a hundred pieces.

'Tell me.'

She did, quietly, although her voice shook a little as he tucked the hair back from her face.

'OK, let's call it in.'

Rafe's influence ensured an officer was on the

scene in record time. Realistically, there was little that could be done other than file a report. The boutique hadn't been trashed, the money taken comprised a one-hundred-dollar float, and she wasn't injured. The fact the intruder had worn leather gloves meant there were no fingerprints. By not removing his helmet he'd made recognition and identification impossible.

They'd run a check, question if anyone had seen anything, but the chance of someone memorising a license plate was next to nil, and the entire episode would end as just another incomplete file.

Rafe saw the police officer from the premises while Danielle collected her bag and followed him to the door.

'I'll see you at home.'

She incurred his sharp glance. 'I'd rather you didn't drive.'

'Why?'

'Indulge me, *querida*.'

'I'm fine,' Danielle insisted, and she was. Despite a niggling suspicion the robbery hadn't been a random act, but a premeditated one with a purpose.

He saw the determination evident, glimpsed something beneath it, and made a decision to postpone pursuing it until later. For now, he wanted her out of here.

There were calls he needed to make to step up security. He made the first from his cellphone as he followed her home, and had the satisfaction of knowing his instructions would be implemented the next day.

Both cars eased to a halt into the spacious garage

within seconds of each other, and Rafe led her upstairs to their room, filled the spa-bath, then crossed to her side.

He tended to the buttons fastening her jacket, and she batted at his hands.

'I can undress myself.'

'So you can,' he drawled, and slid the jacket from her shoulders before reaching for the zip at her waist.

'We'll be late for dinner.' As a protest, it was feeble.

'So, we'll be late.'

The skirt fell to the carpet, closely followed by her half-slip and briefs. He unclasped the clip on her bra, then cupped each breast and brushed a thumb pad back and forth across the nipple.

Her flesh responded, heating to his touch, and sensation quivered deep inside, piercing in its intensity.

She could close her eyes and willingly go wherever he chose to lead.

Without a word he divested his clothes, and her eyes darkened, their dilation almost total.

The breath hissed between his teeth as he caught sight of the long scratch on her inner thigh, and she glimpsed white-hot rage as he sought to bank it down.

'The scissors slipped when I cut through the tape.'

His eyes narrowed. 'Did he touch you?'

'Not in the way you mean.' The fact he could have sent shivers scudding down her spine.

Rafe led her into the *en suite*, closed the taps, activated the jets, and stepped into the spa-bath to settle her in front of him.

There was something incredibly sensual in being

bathed by a lover. The smooth slide of soap-slicked hands over her skin, the light perfume that rose with the steam, teasing her nostrils, the touch of his lips at the sensitive curve between her neck and shoulder.

It was heaven to lean back against him, to let her lashes drift down, and just *be*.

She felt him move, then a brush stroked gently through the length of her hair, and she murmured her appreciation.

After he was done he massaged her shoulders, the kinks she hadn't realised were there, then he turned her round to face him and kissed her.

There was no demand, little hunger…just an open-mouthed gentleness that made her want to weep.

Danielle moved in close and wound her arms around his neck, needing the reassurance, the warmth and heat of him.

To be treasured, loved, adored by this man was not something he offered. But for now, what she had was enough. To long for more was a foolishness she couldn't afford.

Slowly she lifted her head and brushed her lips lightly against his own. Her smile held genuine humour as she rose to her feet and stepped out from the bath. 'Have you forgotten we're due to put in an appearance at Daktar's exhibition?'

'I'll phone and cancel.'

Danielle pressed a finger to his mouth. 'I'd like to attend.'

'Are you going to tell me why?'

He was too clever by half. 'I could be wrong.'

'And if you're not?'

She snagged a towel and wound it round her slender curves, aware Rafe closely followed her actions.

'I need to deal with it.'

She would, but with considerable help, he determined as he followed her into the bedroom and began to dress.

Tomorrow there would be security cameras installed in front and out back of the boutique. As well as an alert button with direct access to a top security firm. What was more, a guard would be present from the time the boutique opened until it closed.

And he'd plan his own investigation. If someone had it in mind to frighten her, or worse, for whatever devious means...they'd pay dearly for their efforts. But first he'd ensure every preventative precaution was in place.

Irrespective of her approval, or otherwise.

It was after eight when they entered the Gallery, and Danielle accepted a flute of champagne from a hovering waiter.

Invitation only ensured the cream of the social élite were in attendance, the women resplendent in fine gowns and displaying jewellery sufficient to warrant the presence of a security guard.

Clever use of concealer beneath her make-up meant the mark on her cheek didn't show, and she'd chosen her gown with care, aware the blush-rose colour highlighted the texture of her skin, the bias-cut design accenting slender curves. Seeking a sophisticated image, she'd swept her hair into a sleek twist, added a decorative clip, and opted not to wear jewellery.

Danielle wandered at will, pausing here and there

to examine the fluidity and style of more than one sculpture which took her eye.

Rafe didn't leave her side, and he made a mental note as she returned to a particular item, a remarkable bronze eighteen to twenty inches high, set against a background of concave mirrored panels, so that every angle was captured.

'It's stunning,' she accorded simply. She could picture it in the boutique. Standing on a marbled column to the left of the counter, set against softly draped silk. It would be a focal point, and capture interest.

She referred to the glossy catalogue and blanched at the price. Perhaps not. She'd need to increase the boutique's insurance just to cover the sculpture's replacement value.

'Rafe, Danielle. How nice to see you again.'

Danielle turned and offered Lillian Stanich a smile in greeting.

'Lillian,' Rafe acknowledged with considerable charm. 'Will you excuse me for a few minutes?'

'He's quite something, isn't he?' the society doyenne commented musingly.

'Something,' Danielle agreed solemnly, and heard Lillian's tinkling laugh.

'You make a delightful couple, my dear.'

'I'll tell Rafe you said so.'

'I'm arranging another fund-raiser next month. I'll ensure you receive tickets.'

'You'll include Ariane in the invitation, I hope?'

'My dear, of course.'

'Thank you.'

'Now, if you'll excuse me?'

Alone, she cast the sculpture a wistful glance, then moved to the next exhibit. Seconds later instinct caused her to glance across the gallery, and there, a striking figure in red, was Cristina.

If the blonde was surprised to see Danielle she hid it well, and after a few seconds of riveting eye contact Danielle raised her champagne flute a few inches in a silent salute, then watched as Cristina crossed the floor.

'I didn't expect to see you tonight.'

As a greeting, it lacked any pretence to graciousness, and Danielle deliberately widened her gaze. 'Any particular reason, Cristina?'

'How was Paris?'

'Romantic, despite grey skies, cool temperatures, and rain.'

'A city for lovers.'

'Yes.'

Cristina took a tentative sip of champagne, then ran a red-lacquered nail round the flute's rim. 'Don't fall in love with him, darling.' The smile became a brilliant facsimile, although there was icy venom evident in those cold grey eyes. 'It's fatal.'

Danielle caught sight of Rafe an instant before the blonde turned slightly and offered him a killer smile.

'We were just talking about you.'

He curved an arm along the back of her waist, and sensed the tension in her stance. 'Home, I think.'

'Cristina would like another champagne.'

'Would you mind, *querido*?'

'I'll summon a waiter.' He lifted a hand, clicked

his fingers, and within seconds a waiter appeared, bearing a tray of drinks.

'Spoilsport,' Danielle murmured quietly, and felt the pressure of his fingers increase.

'Shall we leave?'

'Good heavens,' Cristina mocked. 'So early?'

'He has seduction in mind,' Danielle declared with a singularly sweet smile, then tilted her head towards him. 'Don't you, *querido*?'

The Spanish endearment held a certain cynicism that wasn't lost on the glamorous blonde, and her eyes glittered vengefully for a second before she successfully schooled her expression. 'In that case, have fun, darlings. No doubt we'll run into each other again soon.'

Danielle watched as Cristina disappeared across the room. She had the beginnings of a headache, and she felt incredibly fragile.

'We've remained long enough,' Rafe declared firmly, not fooled in the slightest, and she made no protest as he led her towards the exit.

In the car she leaned back against the head-rest and closed her eyes, glad of the dim interior as Rafe eased into the flow of traffic and headed home.

Fifteen minutes later she entered the bedroom and began to undress, aware of his close scrutiny as he discarded his jacket, his tie, and began unbuttoning his shirt.

'Would you care to tell me what that was all about?'

'No,' she said simply. She walked into the *en suite*,

removed her make-up, her briefs and bra, then pulled on a T-shirt.

When she emerged he offered her a glass filled with water and two tablets. 'Take these, and get into bed.'

Her head felt as if it didn't belong to her body, and she swallowed the medication, then slid in between the sheets.

The last thing she remembered was Rafe switching off the light, the room's darkness, and the relief of blissful oblivion.

Breakfast was a leisurely meal eaten out on the terrace, and, at Rafe's insistence, Danielle rang her mother and relayed what had happened the previous evening, listened to Ariane's shocked incredulity, and gave what reassurance she could.

'Yes, of course I'll be in this morning,' she declared before replacing the receiver.

'I've organised for a security firm to install a state-of-the-art system in the boutique,' Rafe informed as she refilled her glass with juice.

Her hand paused, and she replaced the jug onto the table. 'Excuse me?'

'You heard.'

'There's no need—'

'My prerogative, Danielle,' he declared hardly. 'No negotiation.'

'The hell there isn't!'

'A team of men are due to arrive early this morning. There should be minimum interruption.'

She felt like stamping her foot in frustration at his high-handedness.

'Are you sure you're OK?' Ariane queried with concern the instant Danielle entered the boutique.

'I'm fine,' she reiterated firmly. She felt like a chick with two over-anxious parents, except Rafe's attention was the antithesis of paternal!

'A few faxes, darling. One from Paris confirming our enquiry, another from the supplier informing a delay with an order.'

'Give me a moment and I'll check the emails.'

'I've just made coffee.'

The electronic buzzer sounded, and Danielle moved forward to greet the man who had just entered the boutique.

His proffered business card confirmed his status with the security firm, and the men had hardly begun work when a smartly dressed young woman entered the boutique, presented her credentials, and insisted she'd been contracted by Rafael Valdez as in-house security officer.

'I don't believe this!' Danielle declared angrily as she crossed to the phone and dialled Rafe's cellphone.

He answered on the second ring, listened to her tirade, then directed with controlled calmness, 'Maris stays. End of story.'

'I don't need a damned bodyguard!'

'Live with it, Danielle.'

'We'll discuss this when I get home.'

'If you wish.'

She had the feeling she could *wish* all she liked, but the result would be the same, and she cursed him afresh as she cut the call.

'I'm conversant with your computerised register,

and familiar with sales techniques,' Maris informed with practised efficiency. 'I can double as a sales assistant, and in this situation I'd advise going for that angle.'

Cut and dried, Danielle concluded, and winced as one of the workmen activated an electric drill.

It was going to be one hell of a day!

She silently seethed through most of it, and by midday she had the explanatory patter down to a fine art when clients queried the workmen's presence.

Not only a security system, but cameras positioned out back as well as in the main salon.

The boutique was, she told her mother, more heavily secured than a bank.

'Darling, Rafe has your best interests at heart. Last night was most unfortunate, but it could have been much worse.'

Dammit, she knew that. And, beneath the anger, she was grateful in a reluctant sort of way.

However, it didn't stop her from launching into a verbal attack within minutes of entering the house.

Danielle found him in the study, intent on figures up on the computer screen, and he pressed the *save* key as she entered the room, then he leaned back in his chair and gave her his full attention.

'Why didn't you consult me?' she demanded without preamble.

Did she realise how beautiful she looked when she was angry? He banked down his amusement and settled in for the fight.

'It's a done deal, *querida*,' he drawled, watching as she attempted to rein in her indignation.

'OK,' she qualified as she crossed to stand in front of his desk. 'I'll go along with the alarm system.' She placed both hands down onto the polished surface. 'I'll even concede to the cameras.' Her next move was to lean forward and glare at him. 'But Maris? *Really*, Rafe. Maris is definite overkill!'

'She's in my employ,' he said succinctly. 'I pay her salary.' His gaze locked with hers. 'End of story.'

Danielle picked up the first thing that came to hand and threw it in his direction, watching with detached fascination as he fielded and palmed it neatly, then placed it down onto the desk.

With easy lithe movements he rose to his feet and crossed round to where she stood glaring at him in open defiance.

'You have something you want to prove?'

'*Yes.* Just for once I'd like to see you diminished in some way.'

He lifted a hand and caught hold of her chin. When had want and lust become *love*? He couldn't pinpoint the exact moment. Only that it had.

'You succeeded,' he intoned indolently. 'Last night. Knowing someone had got to you. Imagining how badly you could have been hurt.'

What was he trying to say...that he cared? The thought almost destroyed her.

For several seemingly long seconds she couldn't tear her gaze away from his, and she stood locked into immobility.

There was something unreadable in those dark eyes, and she felt her anger deflate. 'I'm sorry.'

He smiled, and traced the outline of her mouth with

the pad of his thumb. 'Yes, I do believe you are.' He dropped his hand and swept it towards a box sitting on the credenza beneath the window. 'Go open it.'

She stood still for a few seconds, unable to wrench her gaze away from his, then she crossed to the credenza and carefully undid the tape.

There was considerable packing, and she took time to distribute the foam chips, gasping almost soundlessly as she glimpsed the mirrored panels.

The sculpture she'd admired at the gallery.

'You bought it?' she queried with incredulous reverence.

'I thought it would look good in the boutique.'

Danielle carefully replaced the foam packing, then turned to face him. She didn't know whether to smile or cry. 'Thank you.'

'I shall see that you do.'

He was teasing her, and she knew it. But it didn't stop the anticipation of the night ahead as she sat through dinner, logged figures into her laptop, then showered and prepared for bed.

It was she who reached for him, and although he revelled in the slide of her fingers, the tentative exploration of her mouth, it was *he* who took control of the pace, *he* who led them both towards a tumultuous climax that left them both bathed in sensual heat.

'Why do you always have to win?' she demanded huskily, and heard his equally husky reply.

'Because I can.'

CHAPTER ELEVEN

'DARLING, you're looking pale,' Ariane voiced with concern a few days later. 'Are you coming down with something?'

'I don't think so. I just feel a bit tired, that's all.'

'Perhaps you're overdoing things.'

Danielle shot her mother a quizzical look. 'No more than usual.' She could hardly confide Rafe kept her awake at night, and most often reached for her in the early dawn hours.

'Is it possible you might be pregnant?'

She went into instant recall on pertinent dates, then slowly shook her head. 'I doubt it.'

Yet she visited a pharmacy, bought a home pregnancy test, and sank down in a heap when it showed positive.

How could she be pregnant? *Stupid question.*

A doctor's appointment confirmed it.

'Eight weeks.'

'That can't be right,' she protested.

'My dear, I assure you it is.'

'But I had a period last month.'

'Did you notice any irregularities?'

Her brow furrowed. It had been unusually light, lasting less than half the usual time, and she said so.

She listened in stunned silence as the doctor offered a medical explanation. Registered the need for blood tests, and accepted the request form. Then she got to her feet and left the surgery with an appointment card held in her hand.

Dear heaven. A child. *Her* child.

The reality hit as she slid in behind the wheel of her car and drove back to the boutique.

She could hardly hide the news from her mother. Ariane had a right to know.

So, too, did Rafe.

Oh, God.

'It's a *yes*,' Ariane deduced within seconds of Danielle walking in the door. 'Oh, darling, what wonderful news,' she enthused, catching her daughter close in a fond embrace.

Is it? She should be ecstatic at achieving the first stage of the deal. *So why wasn't she?*

Because it meant there was now a firm time-limit fixed on the length of her marriage.

'Are you going to ring and tell Rafe?' Ariane queried gently, witnessing her daughter's conflicting emotions.

'I'll wait until tonight.'

It would give her some breathing space, although the day was pleasantly busy and allowed her little time to think.

Which was probably just as well, she determined as she entered the house shortly before six.

In normal circumstances, she would have booked a table at a favoured restaurant and relayed the news over fine food, wine and candlelight.

Instead, she mentally tussled with words all through dinner and gave up trying to find the right ones as she pushed away a half-eaten plate of seafood paella.

'Not hungry?' Rafe posed, watchful of her desultory efforts.

'Not really.' *Tell him.*

'Something is bothering you?'

There was never going to be the *right* time. 'I had an appointment with the doctor today. I'm pregnant.' There, it was done.

Something flared in his dark eyes, then he banked it down. 'I assume you have a due date?'

Conception had occurred within ten days of their marriage. 'Mid-July.' She managed a smile, although it didn't quite reach her eyes. 'Stage one is now complete.'

He was silent for a few seemingly long seconds, and his gaze seemed to sear her soul. 'How do you feel?'

Oh, my. How did she answer that? Flippancy came to mind, but she chickened out at the last second. 'Fine.'

'You will, of course, transfer to the care of an obstetrician, and cut down your hours at the boutique.'

'No.'

He didn't move, but he assumed a dangerous stillness that succeeded in sending an icy shiver down the length of her spine. 'No?'

How could a single word have the potential to initiate so much havoc?

'I'm young and healthy,' Danielle qualified reasonably. 'If the GP indicates I require specialist care, then so be it.' She drew a calming breath and released it.

'As to the boutique...I intend working right up to the last few weeks.' A spark of anger lit her eyes. 'It's my body, and my child. At least at this stage we're inseparable.' She had to get away from him, albeit temporarily, and she rose to her feet, intent on putting as much distance between them as possible.

His hand snaked out and snagged hers before she had a chance to move more than a single step.

'Let me go.' It was a plea wrenched from the depths of her heart, and one he chose to ignore as he pulled her close.

'Your body, my seed,' Rafe declared with chilling softness. He brought her hand over her stomach and covered it with his own. '*Our* child.'

How could he say that? Already the foetus was a living entity she'd carry in her womb for another seven months, nurture and love every day of its infant years...only to have to step back and share a small part of its life.

As crazy as it seemed, she was already contemplating her separation from a child who had yet to be born.

And Rafe...how could she bear to have him walk away from her, stand by and watch him remarry, provide step-siblings for *their* child, and lead a life totally separate from her own?

Worse, how could she possibly exist without him? *Dear God.*

Realisation hit with shattering impact. *Love?* She couldn't have fallen in love with him. It wasn't possible. Dammit, *love* didn't form any part of the deal!

It had to be hormones wreaking havoc, one part of

her brain rationalised, while another part silently
wept.

'I'll cancel out of tonight.'

She heard the words and felt her stomach plummet.
Opening night at the theatre where actors would por-
tray their parts in a prominent Australian playwright's
new play. How could she have forgotten?

The thought of dressing up and playing the social
game left her less than enthused. However, it was a
prestigious event and their absence would be noticed.

'Why? Pregnancy doesn't suddenly make me a
fragile flower.'

The musing warmth of his smile could have melted
her heart, and almost did. Her mouth trembled slightly
as he pressed his lips to her forehead.

'I didn't imagine for a moment that it would.'

They entered the auditorium ten minutes before the
first act was due to commence. Tickets had been sold
out well in advance, and it appeared many notable
patrons of the arts were in attendance.

Danielle was supremely conscious of Rafe's close
proximity as they mixed and mingled.

'Rafe. Danielle. I was hoping you'd make it.'

Oh, Lord. Cristina. Looking, Danielle had to admit,
absolutely stunning in an ivory silk gown. Her male
companion wasn't someone she'd seen before, and
she banked down the uncharitable thought the blonde
might have rented him for the night.

'I believe we're seated together.'

No small feat in the manipulation stakes, Danielle
accorded silently. Fortunately the electronic buzzer

sounded, signalling patrons to take their seats, and she was saved from having to make polite conversation.

Naturally Cristina managed to seat herself next to Rafe, and Danielle stifled murderous thoughts as she took the seat to the left of him.

He caught hold of her hand and threaded his fingers through her own, and didn't even wince as she dug her nails into his palm.

The orchestra began, the lights dimmed, and the curtain lifted in a majestic sweep.

Danielle attempted to pull her hand free without success, and she fixed her attention on the stage, focusing on the actors who entered it.

Three acts, two intermissions. During the first intermission she excused herself and utilised the powder room. Something for which she seemed to have developed a more frequent need of late.

When she emerged it was to discover Cristina deep in conversation with Rafe. Although, to be fair, the blonde was doing all of the talking.

Danielle joined them, and her eyes widened slightly as Rafe caught her hand and lifted it to his lips.

'What are you playing at?' she demanded in a quiet voice as they traversed the carpeted aisle to resume their seats.

'Reassurance.'

'Yours, or mine?'

The second act captured her attention. Well, most of it. She was too aware of Cristina's possible machinations, and pride forbade she check if the blonde's lacquered nails were resting on any part of Rafe's anatomy.

A further need to utilise the powder room during the second intermission caused Danielle to wonder if a weak bladder was a pregnant woman's curse. She would, she decided, have to buy a book and become acquainted with all the facts!

Fortunately there wasn't much of a queue, and she emerged to discover Cristina making a play at refreshing her make-up in front of the long mirrored wall.

There had to be a purpose for the blonde's presence, and a single guess at the cause was one too many.

Why waste time? 'Presumably it isn't coincidence you followed me in here?'

'It would be a pity if La Femme suffered a few setbacks.'

'Is that a threat, Cristina?' Danielle took a moment to apply colour to her lips, then she capped the tube and tossed it into her bag. 'If so, I'll ensure you're first on the list when the police investigate any further problems.' She paused fractionally. 'It might pay you to remember it's Rafe who owns La Femme, and his connections.'

'Darling, I haven't a clue what you're talking about.'

'No?'

Cristina's eyes narrowed. 'You're a little pale, darling. Not feeling well?'

'I've never felt better.' An extension of the truth, but she was entitled to bend the rules a little.

'One might think—' She came to a halt, her eyes widened, then narrowed down. 'You're not pregnant?'

'Actually, *yes*.'

Cristina's features displayed a gamut of emotions, none of which was attractive. 'Why, you *bitch*.'

'Not the most pleasant manner in which to offer congratulations.' The outer door opened, and Danielle took the opportunity to escape.

Rafe was immersed in conversation with Lillian, and it was something of a relief to hear the buzzer signalling a return to their seats.

'You were gone a while.'

'The powder room is a popular place.'

The lights dimmed, the orchestra began, and the final act got underway.

It was late when they returned home, and Danielle smothered a yawn as she ascended the stairs. It had been all she could do to remain awake during the third act, and as soon as she reached their room she shed the elegant amethyst silk evening suit, removed her make-up, and crept into bed.

'Tired?' Rafe queried as he drew her close, and at her murmured affirmative he brushed his lips to her temple, then prepared to sleep.

It was a beautiful day, with only the merest drift of cloud to mar the azure sky.

Danielle made a mental note to ring the supplier as she eased the car out of the driveway and headed towards Toorak Road. A newly released style of matching bra and briefs was proving popular, and she needed to increase La Femme's existing order.

All of a sudden a streak of blue appeared in her

peripheral vision, she heard the sickening jolt of metal against metal and she was flung forward.

It happened so unexpectedly, so quickly, she didn't have a chance to *think*, let alone brace herself. Although she must have instinctively stamped on the brake, for seconds later the car jumped the kerb and came to a halt a mere whisper away from one of several large trees lining the avenue.

Hell.

She sat there shaken for all of a few seconds, then reality hit, and she reached for the seat belt, released it, and slid out from behind the wheel.

There was concern for the other driver, a need to check damage to her car, and details…she'd need to record details for insurance, log in a call to the police…

'Are you all right?'

Danielle heard a male voice, had the same query echoed by another, and looked round for the other car. Which was nowhere in sight.

'Hit and run,' someone said, adding a vehement, 'Bastard.'

Disbelief clouded her features. 'You're kidding me, right?'

'I think you should sit down, miss.'

Before I fall down? Heavens, I'm made of stronger stuff than that, she wanted to assure, except shock temporarily robbed her of her voice.

'I'll call the police.'

'And the ambulance.'

'I don't need an ambulance,' Danielle protested,

and extracted her cellphone. She should call Ariane and explain she'd be late.

'Stay exactly where you are,' her mother instructed after demanding to know of any injuries. 'I don't give a damn if the car is driveable. Don't you dare move.'

'I'm—' *Fine*, she'd been about to add, except Ariane had already cut the connection.

The rear end of the BMW looked incredibly normal, and there didn't even appear to be so much as a scratch on the bumper.

A police car cruised to a halt, its lights flashing, bare seconds ahead of Rafe's Jaguar, and Danielle momentarily closed her eyes against the sight of him.

A tall, dark angel, she accorded seconds later as he leapt from the car ready to tear someone apart.

As long as it wasn't *her*.

Rafe reached her first, uncaring that he'd broken the speed limit getting here, or that he'd pulled to a screeching halt and caused the cop to pause mid-stride, turn, and check him out.

He completely ignored the steely-eyed appraisal, and if there was going to be any verbalised caution he'd deal with it later.

For now his total focus was Danielle. Dear God, if anything had happened to her... He closed his eyes against such an anguished visage.

It helped to put his hands on her. The instinctive reassurance of touch, and he didn't give a damn who saw him cradle her face and angle his mouth down over her own.

His own reassurance level moved up a notch at her initial response, and it rose a little higher as she pulled out of his grasp. Not that it did her much good, for he merely reined her in again.

'Must you?' Danielle hissed in protest.

His eyes were incredibly dark, his features etched as if from stone as he searched her face. A muscle bunched at the edge of his jaw, then relaxed as his mouth partly slightly, and the tension that had wound through his body like a steel coil from the instant he'd taken Ariane's call began to dissipate.

'Yes.'

She glimpsed something evident she was afraid to define, and for a heart-stopping second everything around her faded as her gaze locked with his.

Did the world stand still? She was willing to swear that it did.

'I need some details, miss.'

And the spell was broken. She turned and saw the uniformed cop standing within touching distance, heard the buzz of voices, and in the distance the wail of a siren.

'I don't need an ambulance,' Danielle reiterated, but no one appeared to be listening. Grr!

With a drawn-out sigh she began recounting the lead-up to the moment of impact...which didn't provide much, for there had been no warning.

The cacophonous siren subsided with a growl as the vehicle drew to a halt, and she suffered a string of questions, contradicted Rafe's assurance he'd ensure she was taken to hospital, then protested volubly as he collected her briefcase, locked her car, and put her in his.

'Just take me to work.'

Rafe pulled out from the kerb, aware he had five minutes before she realised he wasn't going anywhere near the boutique.

She reacted pretty much as he expected, and he reached out, caught hold of her hand and lifted her fingers to his lips. 'Shut up.'

If he thought that gentle salutation was going to win her over, he had another think coming. 'There is nothing wrong with me!'

He spared her a quick, controlled smile. 'Humour me.'

Danielle drew in a deep breath, then released it. 'Where are we going?'

'We're nearly there.'

There was an exclusive private hospital, geared in advance to admit Danielle d'Alboa Valdez into a private suite.

'This is ridiculous,' she flung in a low undertone as she was instructed to undress and get into bed. She cast Rafe a dark look as he prowled the room, and she checked out the cotton gown. Ties to the front, or back? Dammit, she shouldn't even be here at all!

'Here, let me help you.'

He was there, unbuttoning her jacket, easing it off and then tossing it over a chair.

'I can manage.'

He didn't take any notice, and she pushed at his hands as he reached for the zip fastening on her skirt.

'You're in my face, Rafe. Go away.'

'Not a chance.'

She was down to her bra and briefs when a nurse

bustled in, and she indicated her underwear. 'Do I get to keep these on?'

'All of it off,' the nurse responded far too cheerfully, and pointed to the hospital gown. 'Ties to the back.'

'Charming,' Danielle muttered as she complied.

Brisk efficiency resulted in what seemed to be a barrage of tests, questions and an ultrasound, followed by a visit from the obstetrician.

'The baby is fine.'

'Now do I get to go home?'

'Tomorrow. We'll keep you in overnight. Rest, observation.'

'Is that necessary?'

'It's a precaution,' the obstetrician assured, and with a warm smile he turned and left the suite with the nurse following close on his heels.

'I think I'd like to be alone,' Danielle voiced quietly. Rafe loomed large in the room, a tall, brooding entity whose presence seemed to swamp her. 'Would you please leave now?'

Rafe turned away from the window and the scene he'd been studying below. There were questions that needed to be asked; answers he would demand. And calls he had to make.

He crossed to the bed, resisted the urge to cage her in, and satisfied himself with a light, sweeping kiss that left him hard and wanting.

'I'll be back later.'

She could only nod in acquiescence, and when he was gone she laid her head back against the nest of pillows and closed her eyes.

Hit and run. An action which meant a deliberate attempt to harm. Cristina? Had the knowledge of Danielle's pregnancy tipped her from obsession into paranoia?

And if so, could it be proven?

The staff delivered lunch, Ariane rang, the florist delivered a floral bouquet with an accompanying card signed with Rafe's slashing signature, and she spent time leafing through a selection of magazines before slipping into a fitful doze.

Ariane visited on her way home from the boutique, presenting a La Femme carry-bag with an exquisite nightgown and negligée set, plus a pair of satin mules.

'For you,' her mother revealed, hiding maternal concern behind a warm smile. 'A hospital gown is not a good look.'

She kept the conversation light, deliberately refrained from mentioning she'd relayed each and every suspicious incident to Rafe together with her own suspicions, and left when staff delivered dinner.

Danielle had just freshened up when Rafe entered the suite, and she didn't resist when he fastened his mouth over hers in a brief, hard kiss. Then he pulled her close and teased her lips with his own, gently with a lingering softness that brought her hands up to link together at his neck.

'Have you had dinner?' A prosaic query which didn't come close to what she wanted to say.

'Later.' He gathered her into his arms, crossed to a nearby chair, then settled her onto his lap.

'Busy day?'

'Yes.' He'd gone into immediate action, called in

a few favours, gathered facts, then arranged a meeting with Cristina, who had tried guile, tears, and followed them with an avowal of undying love. His response had been a chilling warning, and the advice to leave town within twenty-four hours or face legal charges.

It was *nice*, Danielle decided, to rest in his arms. She could feel the reassuring thud of his heartbeat, smell the exclusive cologne he preferred to use, and sense the clean male scent of him mingling with body warmth to create an essence that was uniquely his.

Perhaps it was delayed shock, but she was beginning to feel quite tired, and a night alone in a hospital bed didn't seem nearly as unattractive as it had a few hours ago.

CHAPTER TWELVE

'WE NEED to talk.'

Danielle had been home an hour, and in that time she'd been plied with tea and bite-size sandwiches.

They were seated on the terrace, overlooking the gardens.

'I have only one question.' Rafe's voice was deadly quiet, his features expressionless. 'Why didn't you confide in me?'

She met and held his gaze. 'I thought I could handle it on my own. What would you have had me do? Run to you, bleating like a baby with every piece of Cristina's nastiness? How was I to know she could be dangerous?'

'If you'd told me of her efforts to cause trouble, her first attempt would have been her last.' He caught hold of her chin and tilted her face towards him. 'And you wouldn't have suffered grief at her hands.'

He finger-combed her hair, lingered at her nape, then he brushed a thumb down the sensitive cord to rest in the hollow at the base of her throat.

The anger left as quickly as it had risen. 'She wanted what I had,' Danielle reiterated quietly. *'You.'*

Cristina had been too clever to show her hand, with the exception that the card she'd expected to play as a *trump* became the *joker*.

Rafe angled his mouth over hers in a kiss that

melted her bones, and it was a while before he lifted his head.

'When I think—'

She pressed a finger against his lips. 'It didn't happen. I'm fine. The baby's fine. You'll have your son or daughter.' And my heart will break when I walk away, she added silently.

His eyes became dark with an emotion she couldn't define. 'You think the child you carry is all that matters to me?' He closed his eyes, then opened them again. *'Por Dios.'*

'We have an agreement—'

'To hell with the agreement.'

'What are you talking about?'

'You.'

She didn't get it. Didn't dare begin to even think he could mean—

'Do you have any idea what I went through when Ariane rang to say you'd been involved in a car accident?'

'I imagine you were concerned—'

'That doesn't come close.'

Danielle's heart seemed to leap to a faster beat.

'Dios. They were the worst minutes of my life.' He slid his hand to her wrist and captured her hand in his. 'If I'd lost you—' He couldn't bring himself to finish the sentence.

She wasn't capable of uttering a word as the seconds ticked by. 'What are you trying to say?' she managed at last.

He didn't try to wrap it up in fancy words. There were only three that really mattered. 'I love you.'

'Rafe—'

'You're more important to me than anything or anyone in my life.'

If only he meant it! 'I think you're in shock,' Danielle said carefully.

'I have something for you.' He reached for his briefcase, retrieved a long envelope, and extracted a legal-looking document. 'Read it.'

She took it from his hand, and skimmed the legalese. There was no need for an explanation. In simple form, it rendered the agreement between them null and void. It already contained his signature and that of his lawyer.

'Look at the date.'

It was dated a day before the accident.

'I planned giving it to you at an appropriate moment,' Rafe declared, and glimpsed the moisture shimmering in her eyes. 'Don't,' he groaned, and watched helplessly a single tear escape and roll slowly down her cheek.

Women's greatest weapon. He gathered her into his arms, nestling her head into the curve of his throat as he held her close.

'The obstetrician suggests a holiday.'

He brushed his lips against her temple, then trailed a path to her mouth, savouring it gently as she began to respond.

'The Gold Coast condominium?'

'If that's what you want.'

She lifted her hands and linked them behind his neck, keeping him there, and it was he who carefully broke the contact.

He'd laid his heart on the line, and she hadn't said a word. For a moment he experienced the agony of her possible rejection. Good sex wasn't *love*. Yet he was willing to swear she cared... All he had to do was persuade her it was enough.

'I think I need to hear you say it again.'

There was no artifice, just a tentative wonderment and a melting softness that touched him in a way nothing else had.

With great care he cupped her face and tilted it so his eyes met hers.

'I love you.'

He thought she was going to cry, and he witnessed her effort to control the tears. Her mouth shook a little, then curved to form a tremulous smile. 'Thank you.'

'For loving you?'

'For giving me the most precious gift of all.'

Something twisted in his gut.

She caught the briefest glimpse of his indecision, and pressed her fingers to his lips. *'You.'* She was sure the warmth in those dark eyes would melt her bones. 'Your heart, your soul,' she said gently. 'I shall treasure them all the days of my life.'

Danielle felt his lips move beneath her touch, and saw the emotion starkly etched on his features.

'At first, I wanted to hate you. For a while, I thought I did. Then I realised the prospect of a life without you would be no life at all.' She trailed her fingers along the edge of his jaw, felt a muscle bunch there, then she traced his lower lip and lingered at its edge. 'I love you.'

His heart, which had been thudding loud in his chest, increased its beat, and for a few seconds he was incapable of speech.

She watched his expression transform, saw the intense warmth, the passion, the unguarded *love*, and there was wonderment that it was all for *her*.

There was also the knowledge she witnessed something she doubted he'd allowed anyone to see in a very long time...raw emotion that came direct from the heart.

He brushed his mouth to hers, then used his teeth to nip the fullness of her lower lip, lingering there before tracing a path to the vulnerable hollow at the base of her neck. And felt the answering kick of her pulse-beat as it moved in tune with his own.

Dear heaven, he had a burning need to hold her, to reassure himself she was alive, and *his*.

Rafe rose to his feet with her in his arms and carried her upstairs to their bedroom. He undressed her with such care it was all she could do to keep the tears at bay, and she watched unashamedly as he discarded his own clothes before sliding beneath the covers to gather her close.

He contented himself with stroking the slender curve of her back, the swell of her buttocks, the toned length of her thigh. His hand lingered at her hip, then covered her stomach, felt the slight thickness at her waist, and he brushed his fingers gently back and forth as if in silent reassurance to the growing foetus nurtured in its mother's womb.

He moved to her breasts, aware from her faint gasp of their sensitivity. Then he kissed her, with a gentleness that caused the breath to hitch in her throat as he began a slow exploration of her body with his lips...

It took a while, and he allowed her to reciprocate in kind, until she reached the most vulnerable part of his anatomy, when he stayed her seeking mouth and turned it to his own in a kiss that shattered them both.

Rafe held her through the night. Whenever she shifted a little he drew her close, simply because he couldn't bear to let her go.

His wife, the mother of his child. His life. To think he might have lost her...

If he slept, he was unaware of the stolen minutes throughout the night hours, and it was Danielle who slid carefully from the bed as dawn broke.

She shrugged on a robe and stood looking at him, drinking in the strong features softened in repose. There was the shadow of a night's growth of beard, and she almost reached down to trace a path across his cheek. Thick dark lashes with their slightly curled edges, and that mouth...

His eyelids swept up in one swift movement, the dark orbs instantly alert, then he saw her and he smiled, a slow, sweet curve that melted her bones.

'Hi.' His voice was a deep, husky drawl, and he extended an arm. 'Come here.'

'You have that certain look in your eye,' she teased, and saw his teeth gleam white.

'And what look is that?' He reached for her, drawing her gently back onto the bed.

'Hmm...dangerous.'

He buried his mouth against the sweet curve of her

throat, and she wove her fingers through his hair, absently finger-combing it as he eased open her robe.

'I can't think of a better way to wake each morning,' Rafe murmured as he bestowed a trail of lingering kisses along her collar-bone.

A delicious warmth invaded her veins. 'This could become addictive.'

'Count on it.'

Later they rose, showered, and took breakfast out on the terrace. It was a glorious day, with sunshine, blue skies and moderate temperatures.

Everything, Danielle thought with satisfaction, was right in her world. She had a husband who adored her, and whom she loved with all her heart. Their baby was growing inside her, safe and doing just fine.

Within a few hours they were due to fly to the Coast for a holiday. Their first together that didn't relate to business.

It would be wonderful, she perceived dreamily as she nibbled toast and sipped from her second cup of herbal tea.

And it was. Lazily spent days spent stretched out on poolside loungers beneath the shade of a beach umbrella. Sometimes they swam in the pool, or walked along the beach, and at night they had each other.

It had all the elements of a honeymoon, Danielle decided dreamily. And there, beneath the warm summer sun, it was possible to believe the past few months hadn't existed, and their lives together began from this moment on.

A trial by fire? Maybe, she conceded. But they'd

forged something very special, and she'd fight to the death to protect it.

The last night of their Coast sojourn was spent lingering over dinner, followed by a stroll along the beachfront in the moonlight.

'Happy?'

Danielle tilted her face up to her husband. 'Yes,' she said simply, and felt his arm tighten along the back of her waist.

He wanted to kiss her, draw her into him, and never let her go.

She linked her fingers with his. 'Enjoying the anticipation?'

'Witch,' he accorded in teasing remonstrance.

'It's part of my charm.'

'I think we'd better head back to the hotel.'

She laughed, a delightful throaty sound. 'Are you going to be this protective right through my pregnancy?'

'Count on it.'

She became serious. 'You won't object if I go back to work for a while?'

He'd been waiting for her to pose the question. 'A few hours a day,' he conceded. 'Preferably mornings, then you can take a rest in the afternoon.'

'OK.'

'Just—OK?'

She cast him a winsome smile. 'Yes.' It was all she wanted, something to keep her hand in. Besides, there was a nursery to plan, baby clothes to buy.

'Such docility.'

'Ah,' she began with teasing mockery. 'The love of a good man can do wonders for a woman.'

His eyes gleamed with humour. 'I think I need to take you in hand.'

'I adore the way you do that.'

'Adore?'

The teasing fled, and in its place was a sincerity that touched his heart. 'I love you. So much,' she added quietly.

'I know,' Rafe said gently. *'Dios mediante, querida.'*

EPILOGUE

JUAN CARLOS RAFAEL VALDEZ entered the world two weeks early, following a long labour which necessitated delivery by Caesarean section. Much to the relief of his father, who appeared ready to tear obstetrician and nursing staff limb from limb, and the bemused acceptance of his mother.

He squalled loud and long, stopping only when he was placed in his mother's arms, whereupon he yawned and promptly went to sleep.

Displaying his mother's relaxed temperament, Danielle sweetly reminded Rafe, despite bearing a striking resemblance to his father.

A comment which earned her a dark, brooding look that couldn't quite reach amusement for the lurking anxiety still prevalent from the birth.

A more doting father would be difficult to find, Danielle mused as she watched Rafe settle Juan Carlos into the crook of his arm at the christening.

In the three months of his short life, their son had become the centre of their universe.

'I think,' Danielle said as she gazed fondly down at her son, 'he needs a sister. Or a brother.' Her lashes swept up as she glimpsed the shock momentarily evident in her husband's features. 'Otherwise he'll be impossibly spoiled.' She offered him a witching smile. 'As an only child, I always longed for a brother or sister.' She paused fractionally, and aimed for guile. 'Didn't you?'

'Danielle—'

His voice was a soft growl which she chose to ignore. 'Can't you just picture a little girl? Lovely dark curls, bright eyes, and the cutest smile?'

'*Amada*, no.' He was drowning here. 'Not yet, I don't think I could bear to—'

'See me in pain?' she finished. 'What nonsense. Women have been bearing babes since the beginning of time. Besides, the obstetrician advised a Caesarean section would be necessary for all future deliveries.'

All? They were going to need to have a serious discussion.

'We'll talk about it later,' Danielle murmured as the photographer assembled them together with Ariane for a family shot.

Later was long after the guests departed, dinner with Ariane had concluded, Juan Carlos had been fed, changed and settled for the night, and they were alone.

'Our time, *querida*,' Rafe accorded, drawing her into his arms. His lips nuzzled the sensitive curve at the edge of her neck, and had the pleasure of feeling her pulse leap at his touch.

'It's been a long day.' A beautiful day, filled with joy and pride, laughter and love. But nothing compared with the love she had for this man.

He was everything she could want, all she'd ever need.

She captured his head and brought his mouth down to hers. 'I love you.'

Her voice was husky with emotion, and his heart thudded to a quickened beat as he slid his hands to her buttocks and curved her into him.

He wanted her to feel what she did to him, to know even on the most base level what there was between them.

His mouth sought hers in a kiss that was surprisingly gentle, until she moved sinuously against him, and then there was hunger, raw, primitive, emotive.

It wasn't enough. It was never enough, and they helped each other shed their clothes, discarding them where they fell.

What followed was a ravishment of the senses, and afterwards they lay curled into each other, spent and gloriously *alive*.

A cry sounded through the baby monitor, and they both stilled as it was followed by another, and soon became a wail.

'I'll go.' Rafe released her and slid to his feet, shrugged into a robe, and disappeared through to the nursery.

He was gone a while, and, curious, Danielle grabbed up her robe and followed him.

There, seated in the rocking-chair, was Rafe with his son cradled against his chest. Juan Carlos had his head tucked into his father's shoulder, and was fast asleep.

'It was wind,' Rafe informed softly. 'I changed him.'

'And found it hard to put him down.'

His smile almost undid her. 'You know me too well.'

'What would the business sector have to say about a hard-headed negotiator known for his unrelenting stance if they could see you now?' she teased.

His eyes gleamed with humour. 'They'd envy me for being one of the luckiest men in the world.' And knew it to be true.

He rose carefully to his feet and transferred his son into the cot, then covered him with such tenderness it made her heart ache.

Juan Carlos didn't stir, and together they dimmed the night-light and moved quietly from the nursery.

In their room Rafe sat on the bed, angling his legs so he could draw her close.

Danielle laid her cheek on the top of his head and wound her arms around his shoulders. 'Are you so against having another child?'

'I think only of you, *amada*,' he said quietly, and felt her arms tighten around him.

'This is a beautiful home, with lovely grounds. Can't you just see three or four dark-haired children enjoying the advantages we can provide for them?' she queried wistfully.

He could deny her nothing. His life had never been complete until she came into it. And love...dear heaven, what it was to love such a woman, and have that love returned.

'A year, *querida*,' he qualified. 'Let us have a year to enjoy our son, before we add to our family.'

She brushed her lips to his forehead. 'Hmm, I love the way you compromise.'

He lifted his head and directed her a teasing glance. 'Only *compromise, amante*?'

She tilted her head to one side. 'Oh, I can think of another thing or two you're quite good at.'

'*Quite*, huh? Obviously I need to work on my technique.'

Danielle slanted her mouth to his, and slid the edge of her tongue along his lower lip, dipped inside briefly, then withdrew an inch or two. 'As in, beginning *now*?'

'Take that as a given, *mi mujer*.' He captured her face in his hands. 'All the days of my life.'

'Only days?'

'Sassy,' he accorded. 'Definitely sassy.'

'But you love me.'

His expression sobered, and the humorous gleam evident was replaced by naked sincerity.

'With all my heart.'

'*Gracias,*' she responded huskily, and leant into him, gifting him everything in a kiss that reached right down to his soul.

There was a part of him that would always be hard and unyielding, but not with her, never with her. She held the very heart of him, and she intended to treat the gift with the greatest of care…for the rest of her life.

The world's bestselling romance series.

Seduction and Passion Guaranteed!

Proud, passionate, primal—
Dare she surrender to the sheikh?

Find rapture in the sands in
Harlequin Presents

Coming soon:
THE SHEIKH'S WIFE

by Jane Porter

Harlequin Presents #2252
Available in May

Pick up a Harlequin Presents® novel and you will
enter a world of spine-tingling passion and
provocative, tantalizing romance!

Available wherever Harlequin books are sold.

Visit us at www.eHarlequin.com

The world's bestselling romance series.

HARLEQUIN®
Presents~

Seduction and Passion Guaranteed!

VIVA LA VIDA DE AMOR!

They speak the language of passion.

In Harlequin Presents, you'll find a special kind of lover—full
of Latin charm. Whether he's relaxing in denims, or dressed
for dinner, giving you diamonds, or simply sweet dreams, he's
got spirit, style and sex appeal!

Latin Lovers is the new miniseries from Harlequin Presents
for anyone who enjoys hot romance!

Look out for our next Latin Lovers title:

THE SPANIARD'S SEDUCTION

by Anne Mather

Harlequin Presents #2248
Available in May

Pick up a Harlequin Presents® novel and you will
enter a world of spine-tingling passion and
provocative, tantalizing romance!

Available wherever Harlequin books are sold.

HARLEQUIN®
Makes any time special®

If you enjoyed what you just read,
then we've got an offer you can't resist!

Take 2 bestselling love stories FREE!

Plus get a FREE surprise gift!

Clip this page and mail it to Harlequin Reader Service®

IN U.S.A.	IN CANADA
3010 Walden Ave.	P.O. Box 609
P.O. Box 1867	Fort Erie, Ontario
Buffalo, N.Y. 14240-1867	L2A 5X3

YES! Please send me 2 free Harlequin Presents® novels and my free surprise gift. After receiving them, if I don't wish to receive anymore, I can return the shipping statement marked cancel. If I don't cancel, I will receive 6 brand-new novels every month, before they're available in stores! In the U.S.A., bill me at the bargain price of $3.34 plus 25¢ shipping & handling per book and applicable sales tax, if any*. In Canada, bill me at the bargain price of $3.74 plus 25¢ shipping & handling per book and applicable taxes**. That's the complete price and a savings of at least 10% off the cover prices—what a great deal! I understand that accepting the 2 free books and gift places me under no obligation ever to buy any books. I can always return a shipment and cancel at any time. Even if I never buy another book from Harlequin, the 2 free books and gift are mine to keep forever.

106 HEN DFNY
306 HEN DC7T

Name	(PLEASE PRINT)	
Address	Apt.#	
City	State/Prov.	Zip/Postal Code

* Terms and prices subject to change without notice. Sales tax applicable in N.Y.
** Canadian residents will be charged applicable provincial taxes and GST.
All orders subject to approval. Offer limited to one per household and not valid to current Harlequin Presents® subscribers..
® are registered trademarks of Harlequin Enterprises Limited.

PRES01   ©2001 Harlequin Enterprises Limited

The world's bestselling romance series.

HARLEQUIN®
Presents

Seduction and Passion Guaranteed!

They're the men who have everything—except a bride…

Wealth, power, charm—what else could a heart-stoppingly handsome tycoon need? In the GREEK TYCOONS miniseries you have already been introduced to some gorgeous Greek multimillionaires who are in need of wives.

Now it's the turn of favorite Presents author

Helen Brooks,

with her attention-grabbing romance

THE GREEK TYCOON'S BRIDE

Harlequin Presents #2255
Available in June

This tycoon has met his match, and he's decided he *has* to have her…*whatever* that takes!

Pick up a Harlequin Presents® novel and you will enter a world of spine-tingling passion and provocative, tantalizing romance!

Available wherever Harlequin books are sold.

HARLEQUIN®
Makes any time special ®